BY MARRIAGE
DIVIDED

BY MARRIAGE DIVIDED

BY

LINDSAY ARMSTRONG

MILLS & BOON®

*First published in Great Britain 2000
Large Print edition 2001
Harlequin Mills & Boon Limited,
Eton House, 18-24 Paradise Road,
Richmond, Surrey TW9 1SR*

© Lindsay Armstrong 2000

ISBN 0 263 16775 5

*Set in Times Roman 16½ on 18 pt.
16-0601-52626*

*Printed and bound in Great Britain
by Antony Rowe Ltd, Chippenham, Wiltshire*

CHAPTER ONE

THE property was called Lidcombe Peace, two hundred acres on the Razorback Range only about an hour's drive south of Sydney city towards the Southern Highlands.

The house, built on a hilltop with stunning views, had been designed with wide, stone-flagged verandas at ground level all around, cream walls and a shingled roof. On this perfect blue and gold summer day, it drowsed stylishly in the sunlight.

The girl standing on the veranda waiting for him was also stylish and looked to Angus Keir as if she belonged to this beautifully established and prestigious property, which, of course, she did—or had. For she was, he guessed, Domenica Harris, whose parents had built the present house although the property had been in the family for a lot longer.

Daughter of noted academic and historian, Walter Harris, and his well-connected wife

Barbara, Domenica had had a privileged upbringing and been to all the right schools, his
research of the family had turned up. And the
only reason she was waiting for Angus Keir,
who had clawed his way from beyond the
black stump so to speak, to hand over the keys
of the property to him, was because on her
father's recent death the Harris family fortunes
had been discovered to be in turmoil, neces-
sitating the sale of Lidcombe Peace.

So he had fully expected to be greeted by a
daughter nursing a sense of grievance, not by
a girl as serene-looking and lovely as this, he
thought wryly as he got out of his car and ap-
proached the veranda; lovelier, indeed, than
just about any girl he'd seen.

She was tall and dark-haired with pale,
smooth skin, a beautifully defined jaw line
with just the hint of a dimple in her chin. She
also had deep blue eyes with impossibly long
lashes and her thick hair was parted one side
and ran in a river of rough silk to below her
shoulders.

She carried a straw hat and a manila folder
in her hand and wore a three-quarter length,

button-through dress in some soft camellia-pink fabric. But the softness of what he didn't know was voile highlighted instead of hid a near-perfect figure and sensationally long, thoroughbred legs. Her flat kid shoes matched the dress exactly.

And for a moment Angus Keir found himself meditating upon the shape of her breasts and the satiny softness of that smooth skin in secret places upon her delectable body.

Then she walked towards him and held out her hand. 'Mr Keir? I'm Domenica Harris. How do you do? I was going to send my solicitor to perform this little rite, then I thought I ought to do it myself. Welcome to Lidcombe Peace and may you spend many happy years here!'

Angus Keir narrowed his eyes slightly. All this had been said in a cultured, musical voice and he'd expected no less. But there'd been no trace of grievance or even regret, and he wondered why the lack of it, in some mysterious way, niggled him.

'How do you do, Miss Harris?' he responded and shook her hand, finding her clasp firm, brief and businesslike. 'It's very kind of you to take the trouble. I hope this is not too painful for you.'

Domenica Harris studied him thoughtfully. Via a real estate agent, she and this man had conducted something close to a war over the exchange of Lidcombe Peace. And it had only been the fact that she'd had to sell some part of the family estate, and sell it quickly or see her mother face bankruptcy, that had finally induced her to accept his offer, which was a lot less than what she'd been asking, although still not an insignificant sum.

Accordingly, she'd tagged this Angus Keir in her mind as a tough customer, and pictured him as a lot older. But he was in his mid-thirties at the most, she judged, tall, with thick dark hair cut short and wearing an expertly tailored light grey suit with a midnight-blue shirt and navy tie. He also possessed the kind of stature that would make him stand out in a crowd, that broad-shouldered, narrow-hipped kind of man who moved with a sort of powerful ease.

But perhaps the most stunning feature about him was a pair of smoky-grey eyes set in a narrow, clever face. Eyes that missed nothing, she suspected, and not the least her own figure.

She said coolly, at last, 'I guess I'm a realist, Mr Keir. Something had to go and this property was an expensive kind of holiday home we can no longer afford. My father, who inherited it from his mother, was the one who really loved it but he's no longer with us.'

'I wondered about the name?' Angus Keir murmured.

Domenica smiled. 'My grandmother was a Lidcombe and her favourite rose was the Peace rose.' She waved a hand towards the rose bushes planted all around the veranda with bees humming through them. 'They're all Peace. We always maintained her preference in roses although this house was built after her death.'

'They're lovely,' he commented. 'I shall endeavour to do the same. So you won't miss being able to spend your holidays here or having a retreat so close to the city?'

Domenica inserted a brass key into the heavy wooden double front door and swung it open. 'A bit,' she confessed, 'but I'm actually so busy at the moment, holidays are not on the agenda.' She smiled ruefully.

'As in?' Angus queried.

She glanced at him, then preceded him into the foyer. 'I design children's clothes. I have my own label and it's finally taken off! I have more orders than I know what to do with and I'm thinking of branching out into women's sportswear.'

Angus Keir discovered that he was surprised. A lovely social-butterfly type was what he'd assumed she was and it occurred to him that perhaps he should have instigated some more research into Domenica herself as well as her famous family.

He said as he stepped over the threshold, 'Forgive me, but I did wonder why I was dealing with you rather than your mother, Miss Harris, in whose name this property is, or was, registered?'

Domenica laid her hat down on a lovely mahogany drum table with a leather inlaid top.

'Both my mother and my sister Christabel are wonderful people, Mr Keir, but not exactly business orientated. Neither was Dad.' She looked briefly sad, then smiled wryly. 'I don't know where I inherited a few down-to-earth, practical genes from, but they're happy to leave it all to me—I have her power of attorney. Now, I have an inventory here,' she continued, suddenly brisk and practical right on cue. 'I believe you have a copy?' She glanced at him out of those amazing blue eyes.

'I do.' He drew some folded sheets of paper from the inner pocket of his jacket.

'And, as you know, while most of the contents of the house were included in the sale, you did agree that we could keep some personal treasures.'

'Yes.' He inclined his head.

'Well, I think we should check the inventory of what was to remain together now, then we can both sign it so there can be no disagreements later.'

Angus Keir looked her over unsmilingly and the nature of the mysterious niggle he'd experienced earlier suddenly came clear to him.

He would like to have some power over this cool, serene and utterly gorgeous girl, some hold, even if it was only that she bitterly regretted having to part with a home he now owned. Why? he wondered. So he could lure her back to it? As an excuse to get to know her? Yes, he concluded, and his eyebrows rose in some surprise at the thought.

Then he realized that Domenica was looking at him curiously, but only because of the lengthening pause between them, and the irony of not making much of an impact on this girl at all when she'd done the opposite to him amused him inwardly but activated a resolve to change things...

'I think that's a very good idea, Miss Harris,' he said. 'And if you have second thoughts about anything you'd really like to keep, please let me know. I'd be happy to accommodate you.'

This time Domenica's eyebrows rose, in sheer surprise. 'That's very kind of you but I don't think there's anything,' she said slowly, as if she was not quite sure whether to believe him.

'Should we start in here, then?' he suggested.

It took them over an hour, and, although he'd inspected the house before and although houses didn't mean that much to him, Angus Keir felt a sense of triumph to think that this lovely home with its use of timber and slate, the design that made the best use of natural light and the wonderful views, was his—even denuded of some of the Harris family treasures.

There was also an air about it of a home, not as if it should grace the glossy pages of an interior design magazine, not matched or co-ordinated within an inch of its life, but comfortable and gracious. Although, he conceded to himself, there would be one thing lacking.

And almost as if reading his thoughts, Domenica said, 'I gather you're not married, Mr Keir?'

'You gather right, Miss Harris, but how could you tell?'

They were in the living room, looking out over the roses towards Sydney. Domenica glanced at him. They were standing almost shoulder to shoulder and, although she was five feet ten, even if she were wearing heels he would be taller than she was, she judged. And his physique and height at this close proximity plus the lines of his face—good-looking but with the hint in the uncompromising set of his mouth and the worldliness of those smoky-grey eyes of a self-assured man who got his own way frequently—did something strange to the pit of her stomach, she found.

He was also tanned where she was not, and it was impossible not to sense that he was extremely fit, and not only from the honed lines of his body but the way he moved. Then there was the masculine scent of crisply laundered cotton, tailored fabric and just plain man about him that was a little heady and, oddly, something rather touching about a small, star-shaped scar at the end of his left eyebrow.

A very fine example of a man in his prime, she thought, but with a slight sense of unease. She remembered, belatedly, what he'd said.

'Uh—' she wrenched her mind from the purely physical '—if I were a wife whose husband had just bought a house, any house, you couldn't have kept me away,' she said with a quizzical little smile, then shrugged. 'On the other hand, it could be easier without a wife who may have wanted to change the house and imprint her personality on it—which could have cost you some more money.'

'I don't think, assuming I had a wife, I would let her change anything about Lidcombe Peace, Miss Harris.'

Domenica's eyebrows rose. 'Really?'

One word but uttered with such hauteur, Angus Keir reflected, he should feel instantly demolished. 'Really,' he agreed smoothly, however, and added, 'I like it very much the way it is, you see.'

'Oh.' Domenica looked around and he could see her doing battle with pride in Lidcombe Peace and the kind of man who would not allow a wife to express her individuality. 'Well—' she faced him again with a fleeting expression in her eyes, this time of 'It's nothing to do with me anyway' and held out her hand '...I'm sure you'd like to explore a bit more on your own, so I'll get going. The other keys are on the hook in the pantry.'

He didn't take her hand but said, 'Would you have lunch with me, Miss Harris? I noticed a restaurant a few miles back that looked rather pleasant. And I wasn't proposing to stay here any longer.'

She hesitated and frowned. 'That's very kind of you but—um—no, I should be getting back to work.' She looked at her watch and then said with a fleeting grin, 'Thanks, but I definitely should be making tracks!'

'You don't eat lunch?' he queried.

'Yes, I do, but on the run, if you know what I mean.' Domenica stopped rather abruptly.

'How about dinner this evening, then?' he suggested.

She was silent, desperately trying to think of an excuse and, of course, every second she delayed made it obvious she had none.

'Unless you eat all your meals on the run, Miss Harris?' he drawled.

Domenica flinched inwardly at the underlying sarcasm of his question. She also asked herself why she was so unwilling to see more of this man without even giving it much thought, and realized it was an instinctive reaction to a subtle process that had been going on between them from the moment they'd laid eyes on each other. Certainly, for his part, an assessment of her that was not only physical but as if her mental processes were on test too had taken place—then again, she hadn't been immune from making assessments either.

But it still came as something of a surprise to her that she should have been drawn into the process. Because she'd been prepared to dislike him thoroughly and with good reason, considering the war they'd waged over the sale of Lidcombe Peace? Only to discover herself speculating on his physique but, not only that, responding to the things he'd said as they'd moved about the house, things that had indicated a sense of humour as well as a man who might be interesting to know intellectually...

Or had it been a lot simpler? she reflected. That there was a magnetism about Angus Keir that could be summed up in three words—sheer sex appeal. It was impossible not to be impressed by his body, by his hands, by an aura of refined strength, as well as touched by the lurking feeling that, when you added it all up, it made you feel particularly womanly.

She blinked surprisedly at this choice of words that had sprung to mind and didn't sound like her at all, and decided it was all the more reason to escape Angus Keir as soon as possible.

She said, 'No, I don't eat all my meals on the run, Mr Keir, but the thing is, although I told you I was a realist, it hasn't been that easy to hand Lidcombe Peace over to you, or to anyone, for that matter, and I think it would be better to make a clean cut now.' Which had an element of truth in it, she mused.

But the expression that crept into those smoky-grey eyes as he looked down at her meditatively was both insolent and sceptical, causing Domenica to feel suddenly unsure of herself. Because he'd read exactly how 'womanly'—just hate that term now, she decided with gritted teeth—he'd made her feel, and knew all too well that she was disseminating for the most part?

Damn him, she thought. Who does he think he is? The Sheik of Araby? Only to close her eyes in further frustration as she wondered where these outlandish or coy expressions were coming from, and to fall back on her mother's tried and tested defence for all situations that she felt were beneath her—pride.

She tilted her chin, looked at him with extreme composure and said coolly, 'So, goodbye, Mr Keir. I don't think there'll be any need for our paths to cross again. My solicitor can deal with any problems you may have.' And she picked up her hat and stalked out.

Nor did she give any indication as she strode to her car of the mixture of annoyance yet skin-prickling awareness of him watching her that possessed her until she was in the car, turning the key. And only then did she give some rein to her emotions—because nothing happened.

'Start, damn you!' she ordered it, and tried again. But it didn't and she only just restrained herself from pounding the steering wheel with her palms.

While Angus Keir, standing on the veranda with his hands shoved into his pockets, grinned satanically and started to walk towards the car as Domenica Harris got out and slammed the door with a lot less *savoir-faire* than she'd previously exhibited.

'It's the starter motor,' he said a few minutes later. 'I'm surprised you haven't had trouble with it before.'

Domenica, still raging inwardly, paused and thought a bit as she fanned herself with her hat. 'Now you mention it, it has been sounding a bit strange lately. Can you fix it?'

Angus took his time about replying because he was laughing inwardly, this time at her lady-of-the-manor manner, and because he knew that, while he might be able to fix it temporarily, he had no intention of doing so. 'I'm afraid not. But I'd be happy to give you a lift into town, Miss Harris.' He wiped his hands on his handkerchief and closed the bonnet. 'The only thing is, I'm starving.'

Domenica regarded him frustratedly.

'I could also tow the car down to the local garage where you could make arrangements for it to be repaired and returned to you,' he added.

She glanced at his vehicle, a large, powerful, latest model Range Rover undoubtedly capable of towing her rather shabby hatchback sedan, and said through her teeth, 'Don't rely on fate always working in your favour, Mr Keir!'

'Certainly not,' he responded. 'But I'm sure you'll feel better after a civilized lunch rather than eating on the run, Miss Harris.'

The restaurant had a garden area with tables set beneath a pergola bearing the weight of a grapevine laden with dark, bloomy fruit. It offered delicious shade on what was now a very hot summer's day, and that was where they ate. There were birds singing in the hedge that screened the road, cicadas shrilling in the grass and yellow cotton cloths on the tables. They also shared a small carafe of the house wine, which Angus had ordered without consulting her.

But, both the wine and the delicious, home-made steak and kidney pie she'd ordered did put her in a better mood. It even made her feel that she'd been rather churlish, and she set out to make amends, although in the most general way. She followed his lead on several topics of conversation ranging from sport, to books, to politics, then found herself, without quite knowing how it had happened, telling him about her business.

'They're girls' clothes,' she said, 'and mar-keted under the ''Primrose'' label. I cater for girls from four to twelve, which is about the upper limit for most girls to enjoy lovely, frothy, feminine creations.'

He raised a dark eyebrow.

She grinned. 'From then onwards they go through a grunge stage or trying to look as adult as possible,' she explained.

'How did you work that out? Market re-search?'

'No. Memories of my childhood and just looking about.'

'So how did you start? With an old sewing machine in the garage?'

'Hardly.' She grimaced and paused as their gazes clashed and she saw a flicker of something that could have been caustic in his grey eyes, although she had no idea why.

She frowned faintly but he didn't explain so she went on, 'After university, where I studied design and marketing, I teamed up with a friend who is a much better seamstress than I am. And, after an assessment of where there might be a gap in the market, we hired a studio and a few more sewers and went into production. I do the designing, marketing and handle the business aspects, she handles the actual making of the clothes.'

'Sounds very professional,' he murmured. 'How did you come up with the capital to start it?'

'My Lidcombe grandmother left me a small inheritance but I also applied for and got a bank loan. That's been paid off, though, I've recouped my initial investment and we're making a steady, although at this stage not exactly spectacular, profit. Since I recently persuaded two major department stores to stock our clothes, which gives us a much higher profile now, and even although we'll need to expand, I expect our profits to rise quite considerably.'

'You sound as if you've got two feet on the commercial ground, Miss Harris,' he commented.

'Thank you.' But Domenica sighed suddenly. 'I just wish…' She broke off and sipped her wine.

'I'd like to know,' Angus said. 'As someone who started off with one eccentric truck way outback, and built it into a transport empire, I applaud your enterprise and common sense.'

But Domenica frowned and forgot what she'd been going to say as something else struck her. 'Keir…not *that* Keir—Keir Conway Transport?'

He merely nodded, although with a tinge of rueful amusement.

'Heaven's above, why *didn't* I connect you with that Keir?' she asked more of herself than him, then focused on him sharply. 'If I'd known that, I would have held out for not a penny less than—' she named a figure '—for Lidcombe Peace.'

'I'm all for knowing as much about the opposition as possible, Miss Harris,' Angus Keir said, 'but it wouldn't have done you any good. I paid what I considered to be a realistic price for Lidcombe Peace.'

She regarded him broodingly. 'I had a feeling this wasn't a good idea.'

'Having lunch with me?' he queried with his mouth quirking.

'Precisely,' she agreed.

'May I offer you a piece of advice?' He was still looking amused. 'Don't regret what's done and can't be changed—that's good personal advice as well as for business, by the way. And Lidcombe Peace was in a price bracket that could have seen you wait for years to get *your* price.'

Domenica pushed her plate away, and shrugged eventually. 'I suppose so. And I didn't have much choice. Oh, well, Mr Keir,' she added in her mother's tone of voice, 'thank you so much for lunch but I really need to—'

'Domenica, don't go all upper crust and la-di-da on me,' he interrupted wryly.

She stared at him. 'I don't know what you mean.'

'I'm sure you do and, anyway, I've ordered coffee.'

She closed her mouth, then opened it to say, 'If you're implying that I'm—'

'Trying to put me firmly in my place? Taking refuge behind a plummy accent and a certain turn of phrase designed to keep the peasants in their place; retreat to your coterie of privilege, et cetera,' he drawled, 'yes. You may not realize it, but it's not only that. You look down your nose and those beautiful blue eyes contrive to look through me as if I don't exist.'

She gasped.

'Moreover,' he continued leisurely, 'I know exactly what kind of a tangle your mother's financial affairs are in, and that the sale of Lidcombe Peace, while removing the immediate threat of bankruptcy, will not solve all her problems.'

She stared at him, struck dumb.

'I know, for example, that there's a mortgage on your mother's principal place of residence that was raised to cover some disastrous investments your father made, so that the profit from the sale of Lidcombe Peace will mostly be swallowed up in repaying that mortgage and all the outstanding interest.'

'How...how...?' Domenica stopped in the act of saying, How dare you? and rephrased stiffly. 'I don't know how you know all this but if you think it makes me *like* you any better, you're mistaken! I—' She stopped exasperatedly as their plates were removed by the waitress and a plunger pot of aromatic coffee was put down.

'It may not matter a whole lot whether we like each other,' he said and poured two cups of coffee.

Domenica's fingers hovered over a little dish of finely dusted pale pastel Turkish Delight that had come with the coffee. 'What's *that* supposed to mean?'

He didn't answer. But his smoky-grey gaze travelled from her glorious dark hair to the smooth pale skin of her throat and the outline of her figure to her waist beneath the camellia voile. She had very fine, narrow hands, he observed, and on the little finger of the hand still poised above the dish of Turkish Delight she wore a rather unusual plaited gold ring. Then his gaze drifted back to her mouth and he contemplated it silently.

Domenica dropped her hand to her lap sweetless and suppressed a tremor that was composed of both outrage and awareness. Because she knew exactly what Angus Keir meant and, while she'd contrived to ignore it until now, one all-encompassing glance from him had spelt it out. 'Liking' one another was not what it was about between them.

Liking one another had nothing to do with wondering about a man on a physical level, which, heaven help her, had plagued her again while she'd watched him discard his jacket to hook her car up to a towline he'd produced from his vehicle. It hadn't been a great physical exertion for him, but enough to make her conscious of the long lines of his back and the sleek, powerful muscles beneath the midnight-blue cotton of his shirt.

And at the garage she'd stood silent and feeling oddly helpless as he'd made arrangements with the local mechanic with the kind of authority, not only of a man as opposed to a woman who knew nothing about starter motors anyway, but the kind of man who almost had the mechanic bowing and scraping.

Then, for some reason, his wrists and hands had specifically plagued her during their lunch. He'd taken off his jacket again and, beneath the cuffs of his shirt, his wrists were powerful and sprinkled with black hairs, but his hands were long and well-shaped and he wore a plain watch on a brown leather band. Strong, but nice hands, she'd caught herself thinking a couple of times.

But she now had to put it all into context, she realized, and find a way to make him believe that 'liking' a man was important, for her anyway.

She compressed her lips and decided to opt for honesty and forthrightness and didn't give a damn how she sounded. 'I don't go in for that kind of thing, Mr Keir.'

'Mutual attraction and admiration?' he suggested lazily.

She paused, then shot him a telling little look. 'Not with people I do business with, no. And not with people I don't happen to like. But most of all, not with people—'

'Men—shouldn't we be specific?' he put in blandly.

She shrugged. 'All right, men, then, who I don't know from a bar of soap!'

'That's commendable,' he remarked. 'I even applaud you, Miss Harris. But I'm not suggesting we leap into bed, only that we get to know each other.'

Domenica felt the surge of colour rising up her throat but she ignored it to say coolly, 'Thank you, but no, and, while you may not be suggesting we leap into bed, it is how you've been looking at me. And I find that—unacceptable.'

He laughed, but with genuine amusement that caused his eyes to dance in a way that was rather breathtaking. 'I'd be surprised if most men don't look at you that way, Domenica.'

Her eyes flashed. 'On the contrary, *Mr* Keir, most men are a bit more...mannered.'

His lips twisted. 'Oh, well, if nothing else, at least you know where you stand with me, Domenica. Incidentally, I believe your mother owns another property, a warehouse in Blacktown?'

'Yes.' Domenica blinked as she tried to make the adjustment. 'It's leased to a catering and party hire company. So?'

'Sell it,' he said.

She did a double take. 'Why? At least the rent provides some steady income!'

'You may not realize it,' he broke in, 'but you're sitting on a small gold-mine there. A new road proposal resuming land nearby has given several companies around you the head-ache of having to put their expansion plans on hold, or move entirely to another industrial es-tate, a costly exercise. But don't sell it for a penny under this figure.' He drew a black pen from his shirt pocket and wrote a figure on the back of the bill that had come with the coffee.

Domenica stared at the figure, swallowed, and, raising wide eyes to his, said huskily, 'You're joking! I know the valuation—'

He stopped her by gesturing a little impatiently. 'Things change. It's an established estate with good facilities and the new road will make it better and even more accessible. And you'll be in the position of being able to play several potential buyers off against each other. Believe me.'

'How...how *do* you know all this?' she asked after a long pause.

He smiled slightly. 'I do my homework.'

'You...*you* wouldn't be in the market for some extra space in this estate, by any chance?'

'No, Domenica, I wouldn't. Do you think I'd be advising you to ask this for it—' he tapped the bill '—if I were?'

They stared at each other, she tensely, he rather mockingly. Until she said a little awkwardly, 'I just can't imagine why you would...just because you wanted Lidcombe Peace...investigate us so thoroughly.'

He didn't answer immediately. Then he shrugged. 'It had some bearing on what I'd get Lidcombe Peace for.'

'You said you—' her voice quivered '—you paid what you thought was a realistic price.'

'Yes. Taking everything into consideration.'

Her awkwardness changed to contempt. He could see it in her eyes and the way her beautiful mouth set severely. And he knew what to expect before she said it. 'That's despicable, Mr Keir. I assume you mean taking into consideration that I was fairly desperate!'

He shrugged. 'Life can be a bit of a jungle, Miss Harris. But if you take my advice on the warehouse, and if you invest some of the profits as I would be prepared to advise you, your mother should be well provided for, for the rest of her life. She may even be able to continue to live in the manner to which she's accustomed.'

Domenica breathed deeply and fought a tide of emotion, an unusual, for her, desire to scream and shout at this man—but what if he was right? she wondered suddenly.

Her mother was one of those people you loved, especially as a daughter—excepting on those days when you wondered why; days when she was impossibly impractical, when she was being a raving snob as if she still queened it over society and had her parents' great wealth to fall back on, when she was unbelievably extravagant. But the thing was, it was impossible to see Barbara Harris unhappy. It was a bit like closing down the sun...

She said slowly, 'I might just take you up on that, Mr Keir. Unless you have a certain kind of repayment in mind?' Her blue gaze was steady, and satirical.

'Your body for my financial expertise?' he hazarded gravely.

'I can't imagine why else you would do it,' she said levelly.

'You could be right.'

Domenica put her cup down and stood up, only a hair's breadth from slapping his face.

But Angus Keir remained seated, with his eyes laughing at her. Just as she was about to swing on her heel, though, he stood up and said, 'To clarify things, Domenica, no, I wouldn't expect that kind of payment. But I would like to get to know you, that would certainly be a way of going about it, and you just might enjoy getting to know me. What would happen from there on—who knows?' He shrugged into his jacket and picked up the bill. 'Shall we go?'

'Your car has been delivered, Dom.'

Domenica looked up from her drawing-board. It was seven o'clock the same evening. She and her partner, Natalie White, were working late although their other staff had left and it was Natalie who was standing beside her dangling a set of car keys.

Domenica looked at the keys then at Natalie, dazedly. 'But it can't be. They said it could take at least a day or two to get the part.'

'Nevertheless…' Natalie grinned '…it has just been delivered by a driver wearing a Keir Conway overall who told me to tell *you* that, on instructions from the boss, he rushed the part down himself, supervised its installation and drove the car back. He also said that, while you should have no more immediate problems with it, it's probably about time you gave some thought to acquiring a new vehicle. Oh, and the bill has been settled, compliments of the boss, too.'

Domenica looked around the colourful chaos of the studio with its big half-moon windows, and said something unprintable not quite beneath her breath.

'Darling,' Natalie murmured, 'I know you explained briefly about this Angus Keir and what you hold against the man, but are you sure you're not spurning a knight in shining armour? When a country garage tells you it could take at least a day or two to track down a part, in my experience and certainly for a car that's not in its first flush of youth, they're actually talking in terms of *weeks*!'

Domenica started to say something but Natalie went on, 'And considering that your hatchback doubles as our delivery vehicle, considering—' she gestured around '—how much stock we have to deliver at the moment and the cost of hiring a vehicle—'

'Stop,' Domenica broke in but chuckling. 'You're right! It still doesn't make me enjoy being beholden to the man!'

Natalie, a five-feet-two bubbly blonde, perched on the corner of a cutting table and studied Domenica thoughtfully. 'I would say this Angus Keir is well and truly smitten, Dom. Is that such a bad thing? Sounds as if he's rolling in dough.' She shrugged and eyed her friend and partner shrewdly. 'What exactly did happen between you two?'

Domenica frowned, because her encounter with Angus Keir had started to take on a surreal quality. They'd said little on the drive back to Sydney, and she'd recovered her composure sufficiently to thank him both for the lift and lunch, although with a cool little glint in her eyes as if to warn him off. But either he'd heeded it or he'd needed no warning off, because he'd responded in kind, and left it at that. All the same, she'd had the feeling she was amusing him and that would not be that— as she now knew.

But even with this reminder—she took her keys from Natalie and stared at them—the whole encounter seemed more like a dream than reality, except for the fact that it had been difficult to concentrate all afternoon because even a dreamlike recollection of events had made her feel restless and edgy.

She sighed suddenly. 'I don't really know, Nat. But for some reason he—makes me nervous.'

She was to repeat that sentiment later in the evening, at home with her mother and sister Christabel.

At twenty-two, three years younger than Domenica, Christabel still lived at home with Barbara Harris at Rose Bay in a house overlooking the harbour.

Close to the shopping delights of Double Bay and because she'd lived there for the past twenty years, Barbara Harris had mentioned several times that she'd die rather than be parted from her Rose Bay home although it was far too big for just her and Christabel.

She'd also tried to make Domenica feel guilty about moving out to a flat of her own several years previously and had tried desperately to persuade her to come home after Walter's death. But Domenica knew that it had been a wise move to stay put because she and her mother were at their best with each other when they each had their own space. Although she often spent the night or the weekend with them and would do so tonight.

Whereas Christabel, who had always been quiet and studious and looked set to follow in their father's footsteps, was able to shut herself off from Barbara's more difficult moods. Still at university pursuing an MA in History, she was also working part-time as a research assistant for a writer, and, Domenica thought affectionately of her sister who was also dark but short, thin and amazingly unsophisticated, she often lived in a world of her own.

Tonight, though, as they ate a late meal together it was Christy who said, 'If he's right and he can give good investment advice, it could be the end of all our problems.'

Domenica grimaced. She'd just passed on the salient points of her encounter with Angus Keir, which had not included the personal, and contrived to strike her mother dumb.

It didn't last long. Barbara reached for her wineglass and said in a wobbly voice, 'This is amazing. This is sensational! I'm saved! Unless—' she looked at her elder daughter piercingly '—there's something you haven't told us!'

'Not really,' Domenica sidestepped. 'I just, well, don't know if we can trust the man, for one thing. For another he did tailor his offer for Lidcombe Peace to suit our rather desperate circumstances and I find that...' She shrugged.

'But if this is true, it's more than made up for it, Domenica. Who is he, by the way?' Barbara asked.

Domenica told them his name.

Barbara looked blank but said all the same, 'I think I'll invite him to dinner. He must have some good reason for wanting to help out and—'

'No—uh—Mum, just hang on a minute,' Domenica broke in. 'Let me check him out first before we plunge into wining and dining him. I'd also like to check out the Blacktown scenario for myself. Please?'

'Well...' Barbara looked undecided and Christy suddenly tapped the table with her fingers.

They both turned to her. 'It's got to be the same one,' she said, frowning. 'Angus Keir, you said his name was, but does he own Keir Conway Transport?'

'That's him,' Domenica agreed a shade darkly. 'Do you know him?'

'No, but I've been researching him for Bob's next book tentatively titled *New Money*. Which he's made a mint of, Angus Keir.'

'Oh. A self-made man,' Barbara said disappointedly and got up to make coffee.

Domenica and Christy exchanged glances, although Domenica was actually feeling relieved, because nothing could dampen their mother's enthusiasm more than 'new money'. But she couldn't resist asking Christy for more details.

Her sister shrugged. 'He was born and raised on a sheep station way out west. Apparently his mother deserted both he and his father, who was employed on the station as a boundary rider and wanted no other life. But Angus broke the mould. Exceptionally bright at what schooling he did grab, he—'

'Started with one eccentric old truck and turned it into a transport empire,' Domenica finished for her.

Christy raised an eyebrow.

'He told me that bit.' Domenica propped her chin on her hands. 'Is there more?'

'He's branched out a bit, he's expanded his business overseas,' Christy said thoughtfully. 'In fact, I would say that Angus Keir knew exactly what he was talking about in regard to the Blacktown property and could probably make Mum a small fortune with the proceeds. But you obviously didn't like him, did you, Dom?'

Domenica looked into her sister's dark, intelligent eyes. 'I...don't know why but he made me feel...nervous.'

Christy considered. 'On the other hand, to know that Mum was happy, settled and back in what she considers her rightful milieu would be such a weight off our minds, wouldn't it?'

Domenica glanced towards the kitchen doorway through which she could hear their mother musically exhorting the percolator to perk. 'Yes, Christy,' she said, 'it would. But, please, just head her away from any plans to socialize with him until I, well, work a few things out.'

'OK,' Christy agreed. 'If she mentions him again I'll tell her he was a boundary rider's son who didn't get to finish high school.'

They smiled ruefully at each other, then Domenica said slowly, 'Not that you would know it—he looks and sounds anything but! Although—' her mind roamed back '—perhaps he does have a slight chip on his shoulder. Do I often sound upper crust and la-di-da?' she asked.

Christy laughed. 'Darling Dom, in fact you're light years from *being* it, but there are times when you can look down your nose just like Mum!'

Three weeks passed, during which Domenica forwarded a cheque to Angus Keir for the repairs to her car and investigated the Blacktown scenario. The cheque came back to her torn up but with no note.

This annoyed her considerably but she decided not to pursue the matter. And, quite irrationally, it annoyed her even more to discover that his summing up of the Blacktown estate had been quite accurate. Through another real estate agent, she found out that the warehouse was, indeed, suddenly a much more valuable property.

She tried to persuade herself that this would have become apparent to her anyway, through offers made for it, but she couldn't persuade herself that she'd have known how much to ask for it.

Then her mother rang one afternoon to tell her that she'd invited a few friends round for a cocktail party early that evening and would she please come.

'Why such late notice?' Domenica asked down the phone, with her mind elsewhere.

'You know me, darling, I'm so scatter-brained, I was quite sure I'd told you about it, then I thought I better check, just in case! I was right.'

'Who's coming?'

Her mother ran through a list of names, and added that she was dressing up.

'All right, thanks, Mum, but I'm so busy, I might be a bit late. See you!' Domenica put the phone down and shook her head. A couple of hours later, she remembered the party and had to shower and change on the run because she was already late.

Damn, she thought as she wriggled into her favourite black dress and did a contortionist act to zip herself up. It was short and fitted, with narrow shoestring straps that crossed over her back, and she embellished it with a single strand of pearls, another bequest from her Lidcombe grandmother. Deciding she didn't have time to fight with tights and it was too hot for them anyway, she slipped her feet into a pair of closed-toed black patent sandals with little heels, and applied some lipstick and eye shadow.

But she hated rushing, she hated being late although she was not a great fan of her mother's cocktail parties, so it wasn't in the best of moods that she let herself into the Rose Bay house, convinced she looked less than her best and feeling quite breathless.

Nor did it improve her mood at all to discover that she'd been right about Angus Keir—he did stand out from a crowd because he was the first person she noticed amongst the throng in her mother's living room.

CHAPTER TWO

DOMENICA stopped dead and looked around wildly, catching Christy's eye in the process. She delicately pointed towards Angus Keir but all Christy could do in return was shrug helplessly in a way that told Domenica she'd also been caught off guard.

And as she looked back in Angus Keir's direction it was to see that he had turned, and, from the mocking look in his eyes as they rested on her, had probably witnessed the little mime between sisters.

Then Barbara was surging towards Domenica, slim, petite and chic in a beautiful blue chiffon cocktail dress spangled with gold swirls that was also brand-new. Not only that, her mother's hair was cut differently and exquisitely styled, her make-up was perfect and her nails freshly manicured, leaving her elder daughter in no doubt that she'd spent hours in a beauty parlour some time today.

But Barbara Harris was obviously happy and excited and as always, managing to infect everyone with her special brand of *joie de vivre*. It was a laughing, light-hearted throng in the room. And even Domenica, who had a very good idea of how much her mother would have splurged one way and another, felt her ire diminishing, although she would have loved to be able to hold on to it as Barbara kissed her and whispered that she was not to be cross because Angus Keir was quite delightful!

Then she took Domenica's hand and towed her across the room to Angus's side, saying gaily, 'Here she is at last, Mr Keir! I knew she wouldn't let me down. Stay put, Dom, I'll get you some champers.'

Domenica took a deep breath and rubbed her nose to make sure it behaved itself. 'Hi.' She contrived to smile whimsically. 'How are you? This is a bit of a surprise.'

'So I gathered but I'm very well, thank you, Domenica,' he returned, looking down at her quizzically. 'Would I be right in assuming you warned your mother off me?'

'Yes, as a matter of fact you would,' she answered ruefully, although still managing to project good humour and taking the glass her mother put into her hand. 'But if I'd known you were here, I would have worn high heels.' She took a sip of champagne and wondered what had possessed her to say this.

Because Angus Keir allowed his grey gaze to wander down her figure in the short black dress to her shoes, then he let it drift upwards again, to linger on the bare skin of her shoulders and the curve of her breasts beneath the fine black material before he looked into her eyes wryly. 'Why?'

'Dom always has trouble finding men tall enough for her, Mr Keir,' Barbara explained. 'I expect that's what she means, don't you, dear?'

'I do!' Domenica confirmed, feeling like a clown but unable to help herself. 'Thank you very much for paying for my car, by the way, but I wish you hadn't.'

'What's this?' Barbara pricked up her ears but was fortunately waylaid by a couple who had to leave early.

And she moved away leaving Angus and her daughter in a pool of silence. He was wearing a dark suit this evening with a white shirt and a plain maroon tie. And there was something about him that made Domenica feel suddenly tongue-tied and oddly helpless, and very much reminded of the three uncomfortable weeks that had passed since she'd last seen him. Because while she mightn't have seen him, she'd been unable to rid her mind of him.

So she stared down at the glass in her hand stupidly until he said quietly, 'You look sensational.'

She raised her eyes to his in some confusion and put a hand to her head. 'I was sure I looked a mess! It was such a rush I hardly had time to brush my hair.'

A faint smile touched his mouth. 'I guess it's the kind of hair that would look gorgeous in any circumstances.' His gaze rested on the glory of her dark hair, then he focused on her eyes. 'Even straight out of bed.'

'It is...' she cleared her throat '...easy hair, probably because it's thick and has a mind of its own.' Then she closed her eyes briefly at the inference of what he'd said, and added barely audibly, 'Don't.'

He raised an eyebrow. 'Speculate?'

She nodded, concentrating on her glass again.

'I've been unable to stop myself from speculating about us for three weeks, Domenica.'

Her lashes lifted and their gazes locked. And her mother's lovely lounge at Rose Bay and all the party-goers in it receded even further as they exchanged a long, straight, telling look. Telling because she couldn't cut the contact much as she might have wished to and, for whatever reason, neither did he. It was also an unspoken admission that, at that moment, there might as well have been just the two of them in the room.

Because all her senses were receiving signals, she thought dazedly. It wasn't only visual, it was much more. It was as if a slow tide of recognition was running through her that told her she enjoyed crossing swords with this man. She enjoyed pitting her intelligence against his, she would enjoy worsting him in a verbal fight, but she would also, she knew, enjoy going to bed with him.

And demonstrating, heaven help her, she thought, that she was more than a match for his sheer, utterly sexy masculinity that no conservative charcoal suit and plain maroon tie could hide.

But just as the colour began to flow into her cheeks at these wild, wanton thoughts that were not particularly like her, Christy came to her aid.

'Excuse me,' she said politely.

Domenica wrenched her gaze from Angus Keir but not before she had the curious satisfaction of seeing him move his shoulders almost restlessly at the interruption.

Then she was introducing Christy to him only to be told they'd already met, and finding herself taking several deep breaths in an effort to compose herself.

'I believe Mum contacted you out of the blue?' Christy said to him in her direct manner.

'Yes,' he agreed. 'She said that, much as she loved both her daughters, she was finding their instincts for caution a little hard to take and she'd be only too happy to have my advice.'

Domenica and Christy exchanged frustrated glances, and once again it was Christy who came to the rescue. 'I guess this all came as a bit of a surprise and that's why we thought we oughtn't to rush into anything, Mr Keir.'

'Of course,' he murmured. 'I quite understand.' But the glint in his grey eyes that Domenica was on the receiving end of said something else—it was unmistakably satirical.

She drained her champagne to stop herself from making any hot and unwise utterances, and replied evenly, 'You were right about Blacktown, Mr Keir, that much I have established, and we're very grateful for it. Whether we—'

'Darlings!' Barbara interrupted, coming back into their midst. 'I hope you're not talking business? I don't think it's the right time or place. Perhaps we could set aside an evening later this week. Would you care to come to dinner on Friday, Angus?' She gazed at him appealingly.

'I would have loved to but unfortunately I'll be in Perth. The following Friday would be fine, however. Thank you.'

Barbara looked gratified but Domenica compressed her lips as he shot her the most wickedly amused glance this time.

'I was wondering if you'd like to have dinner with me later this evening, though, Domenica?' he continued. 'We could discuss Blacktown further in the meantime.'

'I'm so sorry—' she spoke without any plan, the words just seemed to come of their own accord '—but I'm otherwise engaged this evening.'

'Oh, what a pity,' Barbara said. 'Well, let's circulate, shall we? Angus, can I introduce you to one of my oldest friends?' And she took him away leaving Domenica staring at his retreating back, and her sister Christabel staring at her.

'So,' Christy said, '*that's* the problem!'

Domenica blinked at her. 'What?'

Christy smiled gently. 'Dom, the air literally sizzles between you two. When I came up, you might as well have been on another planet.'

Domenica's lips parted incredulously, then she took hold to say a little grimly, 'Chris, the man rubs me up the wrong way and now Mum is calling him Angus and he's calling her Barbara!'

'I think I know why he rubs you up the wrong way.'

Domenica gazed at her sister. 'You do?'

'Uh-huh. He's not your type of man. You generally go for—' Christy gestured '—more...more diffident men.'

'I—do?'

Christy smiled a little wryly. 'You must admit you like to be in control of yourself, Dom. You always have. That's why you and Mum clash sometimes, it's why you've had the single-mindedness to make a success of Primrose, it's why you sometimes come across as a bit high and mighty. But, so far as your love life goes, I don't think it's been such a good policy for you.'

Domenica reached dazedly for another glass of champagne from a nearby table and regarded her little sister rather as an owl awoken in the middle of the day might. 'And I thought you lived in a world of your own, Christy,' she marvelled. 'How long have you been cherishing these sentiments about me?'

This time Christy grinned impishly. 'A few years,' she confessed. 'But I wouldn't have said anything if I hadn't seen you and Angus Keir striking sparks off each other and I'm only saying it now because I don't think it's ever happened to you before and—' she broke off and grimaced warily '—well, you could regret it if you don't go for it—I think you deserve to live a bit.'

'So does he—think that,' Domenica commented a bit grimly.

'There you go, then. It has been tough and you have been such a rock since Dad died.'

'No, Christy, there I do not go. If it had come up any other way—' Domenica shrugged '—who knows? But in *these* circumstances, it's a bit like being held to ransom.'

'Oh, well. But he is rather gorgeous.'

Christy's sentiments stayed with Domenica for the next half-hour, causing her to be a little preoccupied. Then something happened that put a different complexion on things. She'd managed to avoid Angus, although it could be seen that he was quite at ease and generating a lot of interest amongst her mother's circle of friends.

But she happened to be standing next to him, although half turned away and talking to someone else, when Barbara's clear tones and perfect diction made themselves heard in a slight lull.

'Keir and, no, I'd never heard of the name either—new money, of course,' she was explaining to someone, 'but you really wouldn't be able to tell he's a self-made man.'

The whole party missed a beat but only for a nanosecond, then it continued to flow but in that second Domenica caught sight, out of the corner of her eye, of Angus's fingers tightening around the stem of his glass, then deliberately relaxing. In the next second, she made a surprising decision.

She turned fully to him and, cutting across the conversation, said, 'I've changed my mind. I will have dinner with you, if *you're* still of the same mind. The only problem is—' she smiled at him charmingly '—I'm starving so the sooner we go, the better.'

His eyes narrowed and he paused, as if debating something, then he said formally, 'It would be my pleasure, Miss Harris.'

It wasn't until they were in his Range Rover, driving away from her mother's house, that they spoke directly to each other again.

'What about your previous engagement, Domenica?'

She ran her fingers through her hair. 'I actually said I was *otherwise* engaged. Which was true. I was planning to do my washing and ironing but there's always tomorrow for that.'

'Believe me,' he said dryly, 'you didn't have to give up a date with your washing and ironing on account of your mother's unguarded tongue.'

'Well, I thought I did, Angus.' She used his first name for the first time. 'I may look...stuck-up—' she raised her eyebrows '—but I'm not really and I thought it was unforgivable—what she said.'

He made no further comment until they were seated in a restaurant of his choice that was renowned for its food. But not only the food was exceptional, the ambience was superb. Each table occupied its own wood-panelled alcove with burgundy banquettes that you sank into against the lovely grain of real leather, while your feet sank into a thick-pile watermelon-pink carpet.

There were wall sconces dispensing soft light and candles on the tables. The napery was white damask, the cutlery heavy silver, the glasses crystal and between their alcove and the next stood a tall porcelain vase filled with arum lilies and lilies of the valley that were delicately scenting the air.

It was, Domenica knew, one of the most expensive restaurants in town. Also the hardest to get into without booking way in advance. Which caused her to wonder if Angus Keir had been that sure of her or whether, because of his wealth and frequent patronage, he was always welcome.

Then he looked at her thoughtfully across the candle. 'Did you really have your washing and ironing on your mind when you knocked me back the first time?'

Domenica had ordered mineral water and closed her hands around the frosted glass. 'To be honest, no. I...' She hesitated then shrugged. 'There are times when you make me nervous.'

'And what do you think I should do about that?'

'Don't rush me, Mr Keir,' she advised, then bit her lip. 'Look, all I'm trying to do is make amends for my mother.'

'Domenica—' a little glint of amusement lit his eyes '—believe me, I'm not that thin-skinned. It really doesn't bother me to be thought of as ''self-made'' or new money.'

She frowned. 'I think it would bother me. And whether you like to admit it or not, I think there was an instinctive reaction.'

His lips twisted. 'You think right,' he confessed, 'but it was very fleeting.'

'I also,' she ploughed on, 'well, some of the things you've said to me plus my sister's assurance that I can be a lot like my mother, or at least unwittingly look and sound like her, have made me feel uncomfortable and as if I was bunging on ''side''. I really didn't mean to.'

He sat back. 'Thank you for all this—' he looked at her gravely '—but if you're picturing me as having an enormous chip on my shoulder about old money and new money, rightly or wrongly, I don't. I'm thirty-six,' he added wryly. 'I've come a long way from the back of Tibooburra—so, yes, sometimes the odd little pinprick touches a nerve, but for the rest I couldn't give a damn. Take me or leave me in other words, but you don't have to go on apologizing.'

Their entrée was served at this point.

Domenica had chosen calamari and it was delicious. She ate most of it while she thought out a response. 'What if I still decide—' she wiped her fingers, 'to—er—leave you, as you put it?' she queried.

'Do you mean what would I think of you?'

'Mmm.' She touched her napkin to her lips.

'I think I'd put it down to a truer kind of elitism than your mother is capable of,' he said.

Her eyes widened. 'What do you mean?'

'That you must think you're too good for me, Domenica, to want to completely ignore the kind of simultaneous attraction we felt from the moment we laid eyes on each other.'

Instead of firing up—perhaps the food and the soothing perfection of the restaurant were having a beneficial effect, she theorized to herself—she sat back and looked around until the next course arrived.

Nor did he attempt to enlarge on his statement or elicit a response but he was completely at ease, she could see, as he lounged back against the leather, watching her.

She'd ordered a fillet steak but she only stared at it for a long moment after it arrived. Then she raised her eyes to Angus Keir. 'How do you know there isn't a man in my life? Wouldn't that be reason enough to ignore you?'

'Certainly,' he conceded. 'Although it would be a bit of a worry to feel like that about someone else if you had a serious man in your life, don't you think?'

She looked at him darkly.

It didn't make any impression because he continued smoothly, 'But there is no man in your life, Domenica.'

'How do you know that—for heaven's sake? Don't tell me your homework extended to spying on my personal life!' she protested.

'Your mother was happy to fill me in without me even asking, as it happens. We had quite a long conversation. I know that Christy is bookish and a lot like her father. I know there have been other men in your life but none too serious. Your mother attributes it to the fact that you have a mind of your own over and above what might be good for a girl.'

Domenica attacked her steak rather savagely.

'You don't agree with that assessment?' he asked.

'From someone who has a mind of her own over and above what might be good for *anyone*, no!'

'I take it you and your mother clash at times?'

'Yes. Don't tell me you and your mother didn't have the odd disagreement—' She stopped abruptly and closed her eyes. 'I'm so sorry, I just wasn't thinking.'

'It appears you've been doing some homework, Domenica,' he said with a faint undercurrent of sarcasm.

She coloured faintly. 'I didn't set out to do it. Christy is a research assistant to a writer who's doing a book on ''new money''. You're to be in it.'

'Ah. What else did she dig up about me?'

Domenica shrugged. 'That you were extremely bright. Have you...' she paused '...never found your mother?'

'Yes, but only after her death.'

'I'm sorry,' she said with genuine compassion.

'She did abandon me.'

Domenica scanned his expression but he displayed no emotion. 'All the same, she may have had her reasons.'

'I'm sure she did. My father was a hard man although a lot harder after she left. But, anyway, let's concentrate on *your* mother. Would you like a glass of this excellent wine, by the way?'

Domenica studied the bottle of red that had come with their main course, and chuckled softly. 'Do I look as if I need it? On account of my mother? Perhaps I do, thank you.'

He poured the wine and they ate in silence for a while.

Then Domenica said slowly, 'There are times when she drives me mad. She knows as well as I do that she's not out of the woods financially yet, but I'd hate to think what today cost her. A new dress, French champagne, et cetera. But if you could see her working with disabled children—she's very musical and she arranges concerts for them—if you could have seen her devotion to my father and if you knew how she worries about Christy and me—more me,' she said ruefully, 'you would have to admire and love her. I—'

'It's OK. I get the picture,' he said, not quite smiling. 'You two would go to the ends of the earth for each other but in close confines things can get a little hair-raising.'

Domenica picked up her glass, sat back and felt herself relaxing. 'Yes.'

'Well,' he murmured, 'now we've sorted that out perhaps we could talk about us?'

She eyed him over the rim of her glass. 'What would you like to say?'

'Would you come dancing with me after dinner?'

She opened her mouth but he broke in humorously, 'No, don't say the first thing that springs to mind, Miss Harris, which no doubt would be a refusal. At least give it a little thought.'

This was an accurate enough assessment of what she'd been about to do to cause her to curse herself inwardly for being so transparent but, not only that, to wonder whether she was being stuck-up again. But dancing with a man was not the same thing as having dinner with him, and surely you were entitled to refuse without being considered a snob?

'I...' She stopped awkwardly. 'Where?'

'Here. They open a disco at eleven o'clock.'

She looked at her watch and was amazed to discover it was nearly eleven now. 'All right,' she said abruptly. 'It's good exercise if nothing

else. And I'll have...' She broke off frustratedly.

'Completely atoned for your mother?' he
suggested.

She shrugged but was unprepared for the
way his eyes danced and his teeth gleamed as
he said, 'I'll try not to make it a too degrading
experience for you, Domenica.'

'I didn't mean that—I—'

'Of course not,' he interposed seriously.
'Especially when you're pulling out all stops
to prove to me you don't consider yourself
above me in any way.'

She set her teeth. Then she put her head to
one side and regarded him coolly. 'I just hope
you're a good dancer, Mr Keir.'

'We shall see, Miss Harris,' he replied formally, but his smoky-grey eyes were still
laughing at her.

At eleven o'clock a set of wooden doors was
rolled apart to reveal an Aladdin's cave.

Domenica blinked because she'd eaten at
this restaurant before but never been to the
disco. So the grotto-like interior with its pin-

prick, jewel-bright swinging lights and pol-
ished floor came as something of a surprise.
Then the music started, more as background
music at first, and she and Angus finished their
coffee leisurely.

It wasn't until there were several other cou-
ples on the floor that he raised an eyebrow at
her. 'Should we get it over and done with?'

A little glint in her blue eyes told him she
resented, possibly irrationally, his implication
that she was about to perform a penance, but
she murmured, 'By all means.'

Ten minutes later, she knew without doubt
that she'd thrown down the wrong gauntlet.
Angus Keir was a very good dancer. So good,
it was impossible, especially if you loved
dancing yourself, to be stiff, and unresponsive
in his arms. Not that she'd planned to be stiff,
precisely. But she certainly hadn't planned on
throwing aside all caution and giving herself
over to the music—and to him. Yet the two
were inseparable. And it occurred to her that,
if she wanted to continue to hold herself aloof
from him and the attraction between them,
she'd made a tactical error.

On the other hand, all her senses were stirring as they moved together with their bodies touching. She felt light, slim and shapely in his arms—his hands on her waist seemed to emphasize its slenderness and her skin felt like velvet beneath his fingers. And the contact with his hard, honed body did strange things to her breathing and caused tremors of delicious anticipation to run through her.

Nor did the sensuous rhythm they were dancing to help matters. It stirred her blood and it came naturally to move with a fluid grace that was both provocative and a celebration of her lithe, tall figure in the revealing little black dress that emphasized the pale, smooth glossiness of her skin. But most of all, even above the sureness of the way he led her and how they moved together in complete unity, the way he watched her was the most worrying.

Because it told her that the provocation she was unable to help herself offering was being noted and could be held against her at some time in the future. But those smoky-grey eyes also blazed a trail almost as tangible as if his fingers or lips were exploring the satiny skin of her throat, the valley between her breasts and elsewhere.

Then the disco changed beat and, with a sheer effort of will, she grasped the opportunity to release herself from the mesmerizing power of Angus Keir and the music. 'I...think I'd like to sit down.'

He didn't release her immediately and she stood in the circle of his arms for a long moment, wondering if she was mad, because it felt so good, to want to rationalize this powerful force between them.

It was the sudden glint of irony in his eyes that told her she should but, not only that, she should take all possible precautions against falling under the spell of a man she barely knew who was also wielding another kind of power over her—her mother's future.

But for a shocking little instant what she really wanted to do, she discovered, was kick her shoes off, wind her arms round his neck and really let her hair down as they moved to the soft but insistent beat of the music. It even crossed her mind that it would be perfect if they were somewhere quite private...

She swallowed and looked away from his quizzically raised eyebrows—as if he could sense everything that was going through her mind. And she stepped backwards, pressing against his arms. For a moment they tightened about her and his hands moved on her hips, for a moment his grey eyes glinted in an intimate understanding of her dilemma, then he let her go.

By the time she got back to their table, her breathing had steadied, her tingling senses had calmed down a bit, but she was grateful for the liqueur brandies he ordered, as well as another pot of coffee.

But when he said, cradling his balloon glass in one hand and looking down at it reflectively, 'This should be interesting, Domenica,' her hackles rose immediately.

'What's that supposed to mean?'

He raised his eyes and looked her over in silence before he said, 'Something went amiss otherwise we'd still be out there but I just wondered where you were going to lay the blame before it did. The music?'

She lowered her lashes and contemplated her options. Make excuses for herself? No way, she decided grimly. So she tossed her hair and looked at him ingenuously. 'I think I'll leave that for you to work out, Mr Keir. But I'd be grateful, when we've finished these...' she waved a slim hand over her brandy and coffee '...if you could drop me home. I am a working girl, if not to say an overworked girl at the moment. Unless you'd like me to order a taxi?'

'Unless you like to play hard to get, Domenica?' he parodied.

She held onto her temper by the narrowest of margins and forced herself to meet his look of scathing insolence, unflinchingly. 'I don't like to repeat myself, Angus, but—don't rush me. This is only the second time we've met but, not only that, it's a little hard to distance myself from the feeling that I could be ransomed into supplying a sort of goods and services tax.'

'I gave you Blacktown free, gratis and for nothing, Domenica,' he replied harshly. 'And you're welcome to take the profits to any investment advisor in town. I have no hold over you if that's what you're trying to say.'

'Only that my mother now regards you as her saviour,' she murmured. 'Only gratitude.'

'Your mother got in touch with me, not the other way around.'

'So you had no intention of contacting me yourself?' she asked.

'On the contrary, I had every intention of contacting you—I've been overseas for most of the last three weeks,' he drawled.

She hesitated briefly, then, 'And what kind of a proposition had you in mind before my mother got to you?'

His grey gaze played over her leisurely—if she'd angered him earlier, it was gone now, she thought, and wondered why that worried her.

'A date—dinner? A movie? A picnic on the beach?' he suggested with sheer derision in his eyes. 'Not—mannered enough for you, Domenica?'

'Not at all.' A faint smile touched her mouth. 'A picnic on the beach, though? A bit of a change from—' she looked around '—this kind of sophistication and being able to walk in here off the street and command a table.'

'I was seventeen before I saw the sea,' he countered. 'For some reason I got tears in my eyes. It was the start of a love affair and I still picnic on the beach when I can find the time— and a deserted beach.'

Domenica's lips parted as her smile faded. And her voice was husky when she spoke at last. 'I seem to have put my foot in my mouth more than once this evening.'

He said nothing.

She blinked a couple of times. 'I grew up beside the sea and never realized how lucky I was. I'd…like to take you up on the picnic.'

'I'm taking the day off, tomorrow, Nat,' Domenica said the next morning.

Natalie blinked at her.

'I know I can't really spare the time…' Domenica looked a little helplessly at the pile of dresses awaiting a final inspection then pressing and packaging, not to mention the pile of paperwork on her desk '…but I got myself into something I just can't back out of, unfortunately.'

'Social?'

'Uh-huh.'

'Not the man on the white charger, by any chance?' Natalie enquired innocently.

'Yes—but how on earth could you guess that?' Domenica frowned at her partner.

Natalie smiled a little smugly. 'You've been a bit vague all morning. Just like you were the day you came back from having lunch with him.'

Domenica ground her teeth.

'So what are you doing tomorrow?'

'Going to the beach but it may pour again.' Domenica looked hopefully out of the rain-lashed windows.

'Not what the weather bureau is predicting,' Natalie said cheerfully and added, 'Don't worry, I'll fix all this.' She waved a hand towards the pile. 'So you don't need to feel guilty or anything; you can go with a clear conscience, in other words.'

'Thank you,' Domenica said, but a little grimly.

The next morning, she opened her eyes to bright sunshine washing the veranda of her apartment, and sighed as she pulled a pillow into her arms.

Because the thought of spending a whole day with Angus Keir was nerve-racking enough, but a day at the beach was more so. Yet she'd been genuinely moved by his confession of what the sea had done to him, and genuinely aware that there was a stubborn, irrational quality to her desire to resist him. Especially after she'd danced with him.

None of it meant that she thought she was too good for him, however. So what did it mean? she pondered. That Christy was right?

She sat up abruptly and rested her chin on her knees. Or that she herself had a sixth sense about Angus Keir? A sense of something indefinable that nevertheless told her to be wary of him. Could it even be a sense that when the high and mighty fall, they fall all the harder?

she asked herself with a tinge of rather uneasy humour.

Then she shrugged and decided all she could do was take the day as it came—and she got up to shower and dress.

At ten o'clock she was waiting for him in the foyer of her building wearing white shorts and an iris-blue blouse that matched her eyes and was unbuttoned to reveal a matching costume beneath it. She also wore navy canvas shoes, gold hoop earrings and her hair was tied back beneath a racy white peaked cap.

She carried a navy raffia holdall and she'd also brought a small cool-box although he'd told her he would provide the picnic. She wasn't sure whether it was in the spirit of wanting to make a contribution or just wanting to be independent, but she'd made a carrot cake, packed some fruit and cheese, a bottle of soft drink and a flask of Blue Mountain coffee.

At three minutes past ten the now-familiar dark green Range Rover drew up outside her building and Angus Keir got out wearing buff shorts and a lime-green polo shirt.

They met on the pavement and it struck Domenica that he had a habit of looking her over unsmilingly—as he did for a long, curiously tense little moment. Then a glimmer of a smile twisted his lips and he put out his hand.

She shook it and said gravely, 'Does this mean I pass muster?'

He kept hold of her hand. 'You're a sight for sore eyes, Domenica. And even the weather, which I was sure was going to obey your caution that fate wouldn't always be on my side, has come good.'

She laughed, genuinely, and couldn't repress the warm little trill that ran through her although she said teasingly, 'You're not too bad yourself, Angus. Have you found us a deserted beach?'

It wasn't quite deserted but being a weekday helped. And the beach was a golden curve of sand backed by green cliffs, the sun was hot and the surf was magnificent.

After their swim, Angus set up an umbrella and shook out a blanket beside a small, rocky headland. And he set out lunch. Cold chicken, crusty rolls, a Greek salad with creamy feta cheese and plump black olives glistening beneath a tangy dressing. There was also an avocado salsa made with tomatoes, chillies, onion and basil. The plates were white melamine, the cutlery had brightly coloured acrylic handles, and the glasses had pewter stems. He also produced napkins printed with sailing ships and a pottery cooler for the wine.

Domenica sat on her towel in her sleek iris-blue one-piece swimsuit, and watched these preparations as she squeezed and combed her hair. 'Very impressive, for a bachelor,' she murmured and reached for her sun cream.

He grimaced. 'I can't take the credit. My housekeeper did it all.'

She smiled. 'So, if it had been left to you, what would you have done to keep the hunger pangs at bay?'

He raked his dark, wet hair out of his eyes and squinted around. 'Hopped in the car and found the nearest hamburger or hot-dog stall.'

Domenica burst out laughing. 'I wouldn't have minded, you know! I've never been known to say no to a hamburger.'

Angus looked down at his repast ruefully. 'Now you tell me. Mrs Bush will be heartbroken.'

'No, she won't, I promise I'll do her meal full justice. I also adore cold chicken and the salad and salsa look divine.'

He sat down and reached for the wine— they'd slaked their thirst with Domenica's barley water as soon as they'd come out of the water. He was wearing a pair of navy board shorts with a red trim and droplets glistened on the bronzed width of his shoulders. There was a sprinkling of dark hairs down his chest and on his legs, and even in repose his body was powerful.

She said, to take her mind off it, 'You swim surprisingly well for a boy who didn't see the sea until he was seventeen.'

He pulled the cork from the bottle with a corkscrew and replied mildly, 'There are dams and creeks in the outback, Domenica. It's just not the same as the sea.'

'Of course.' She looked uncomfortable.

'So do you, incidentally—swim well.' He poured two glasses of wine.

She was silent as she accepted hers and sipped it.

'Have I said something wrong?' he asked after a few minutes.

'No.' She shrugged. 'I just seem to *keep* putting my foot into things.'

His grey eyes narrowed on her and his lips twitched. 'Why don't we take another tack, then? Let's not *try* to make conversation or keep things merely *pleasant* between us.'

She blinked. 'Is that what you think I'm trying to do?'

He put his glass down and dished up some chicken and salad for her, and he didn't respond in kind, just glinted a keen little glance her way.

She took her plate and thanked him, then sighed suddenly. 'I don't seem to know where to start. I was going to ask you if you've stayed at Lidcombe Peace but even that is fraught with innuendo.'

'I'm moving in the weekend after next.'

'So—you're going to live there? Full-time, I mean?'

'Why should that surprise you?' he asked.

'I don't know,' she confessed and waved the chicken leg she was eating with her fingers. 'For such a consummate businessman, I thought you'd prefer to live in the city, I guess.'

'I'll still have a place in the city and I'll still spend most of the week in town but, forgive me—' he looked at her humorously '—those acres of Lidcombe Peace are crying out to be made some use of. So I'm going to improve the pastures and breed stud cattle, amongst other things. Which means new fencing, dams, et cetera. I also plan to keep a few horses and I may branch out into alpaca farming. Do you ride, by the way?'

'Yes,' she said enthusiastically.

He paused and looked down at his plate, then went on thoughtfully, 'You see, these days, you can virtually run a business at the touch of a button. And Lidcombe Peace, for someone like me, who was brought up to huge distances, is only a stone's throw from my headquarters anyway. But I've reached the stage in my life when I need something else to do as well as make money.'

'I'm...' Domenica studied him seriously '...happy to hear that!'

He looked up at last, wryly. 'The money bit?'

'No.' She waved her drumstick again. 'My Lidcombe grandmother did run cattle there and, while my father did love the place, she always used to bemoan the fact that he let that side of things slide. I think she'd be delighted to hear your plans for it. So, there's still something of the land in your blood, Angus?'

'Apparently,' he murmured. 'There were two things I did well: rounding up sheep on horseback and understanding the mechanics of car motors.'

'That's not quite what I heard—' Domenica stopped and frowned. 'Yet you couldn't start my car three and a half weeks ago?'

'Well...' he finished his lunch and put his knife and fork together '...as a matter of fact I could have, temporarily.'

'Then why didn't you?' Her expression was haughty.

He looked humble but utterly falsely so—if you were beginning to get to know the different glints in his eyes. 'Sorry, ma'am—'

Domenica clicked her tongue frustratedly. 'Don't start that again!' she warned.

'I thought it might have been the other way around but,' he said hastily, 'had you, for any reason, had to stop the motor on your way back, you may have still been in the same spot. Although that wasn't my main reason.'

A look of utter exasperation chased across Domenica's face.

'I wanted to have lunch with you, that's all,' he said simply.

'As in all's fair in love and war—I mean, does that explain why you're looking particularly smug at the moment, Angus Keir?' she queried ominously.

'Well—' he scanned her from head to toe '—put it this way, you look like a particularly lovely although rather stern mermaid at the moment, who is quite capable, however, of luring me to my—undoing.'

She relaxed unwittingly, she just couldn't help herself, although she said, 'That kind of talk will get you nowhere!'

'Would you come down and spend a week-end at Lidcombe Peace with me, Domenica?'

She stilled utterly; her breathing even seemed to suspend itself for a fleeting second.

'Would it be that painful?' he queried. 'To see it as your grandmother wanted it to be?'

'Would that be your only motive in asking me, Angus?' she responded at last.

'No. I could dine you and wine you, not to mention dance with you until the cows come home or even bring you to the beach...' he looked around '...but with a project that's dear to your heart, with horses to ride and a wonderful place to do it, we could get to know each other in a different, less superficial way.'

CHAPTER THREE

THE tide was going out, leaving a silver tracery on the sand, and the surf was gentler. Some expectant seagulls were hovering for titbits and squabbling amongst themselves as they jockeyed for positions. Domenica watched their red legs and beady eyes and felt the heat of the day, almost like a cloak, on her skin. The beach was now deserted except for one lone fisherman and even he was packing up to go home.

Siesta time, she thought, except for ever-hungry seagulls, and with an effort raised her gaze to Angus Keir's.

'You don't think your real motivation could be to make you feel like the lord of the manor at the same time as you set out to seduce me in my old home?' she asked.

'Seduce you?' he said sceptically. 'How? By force?'

'How would I know if that's not how you like to get your kicks, Angus?' she answered tautly. 'But—'

'I'll tell you,' he interposed, with a scathing look of condemnation in his eyes. 'You'd have read about it in the paper. I'd be in jail if that's how my tastes ran.'

She gestured frustratedly, and with an undercurrent of embarrassment she couldn't quite hide. 'Even so—all right! That may have been uncalled for,' she conceded, 'but, apart from anything else, why do a man and a woman spend a weekend together? And don't you think it would reawaken some memories I'd prefer to forget—going back to Lidcombe Peace?'

'Not if you're the realist you claim you are, Domenica. But I have to doubt that assessment of yourself on at least two fronts now. This persistent wish to dissociate your mind from what your body tells me being one of them.'

She got to her knees and put her hands on her hips. 'Do you know why I came today?'

'I can guess,' he drawled, stretching his legs out and propping his head negligently on one elbow. 'To pat me on the head because you felt a little sorry for an underprivileged boy who got tears in his eyes at the sight of the sea but, principally, to prove how unaffected you could be by the physical, sensuous reaction we share towards one another.'

She gasped.

'And yes—' he sat up and captured her outraged blue gaze '—I think I would enjoy being lord of the manor at Lidcombe Peace, but only because I've never before encountered the purely patronizing manner you display so effectively, Domenica Harris.'

She shot to her feet, closing her mouth with a click, then opened it, but before she could marshal her thoughts he stood up outside the circle of the umbrella and pulled her into his arms.

'Don't tell me,' he said barely audibly as she was momentarily stunned into offering no resistance, 'we haven't been mentally circling every damn thing about each other from the time we took our clothes off.'

The tide of colour that poured into her cheeks told its own tale.

He smiled but not amusedly. 'And don't tell me it doesn't feel good for both of us, to be in each other's arms like this instead of torturing ourselves with the mental images of it.'

Every sane, rational ethic she possessed told Domenica to deny this charge. She even started to say that, far from being in each other's arms, she was in *his* arms but not by choice. Then it occurred to her she was no prisoner and the only reason she couldn't simply walk away was because some strange fascination within her refused to let her.

The same thing, only muted, that had warmed her when she'd first laid eyes upon him, tall, dark and good to look upon in his shorts and lime-green shirt, this morning. The same fascination that had flared up between them two nights ago was lighting her senses once again, only now she had less than her little black dress to shield her. And he had less to hide how streamlined and strong he was, how brown and essentially masculine.

But why *so* spellbinding? she found herself wondering wildly. So unlike what any man had ever done to her before. So that her heart was racing as his hands moved up from her waist towards her breasts beneath her swimsuit, her pulses were hammering but with the next thought springing to mind being—this will do it! Surely no man could touch her like this against her will without—what?

Drawing a response from her that was instinctive and even made her gasp with delight, she discovered. Because those strong, nice hands were also wise and gentle, she found. And they could dispense sensations that washed through her like waves of pure pleasure. Then he took his hands away and pulled her into his arms again, and she heard him say her name unevenly into her hair. One word, she marvelled, but it made it feel like the most natural thing in the world, when his lips sought hers then, to surrender to his kiss with undisguised rapture.

A clap of thunder finally drew them apart, then the odd raindrop but stinging like a missile, started to fall on them, and for a moment they could both only stare upwards at the black storm-tossed clouds above them in genuine disbelief.

Until he stepped back from her and said wryly, 'I rest my case.'

She closed her eyes briefly and turned away from him. But before either of them could add anything it started to pour and lightning flashed across the clouds in brilliant zigzags.

With one accord, they packed up as best they could, gathered everything they could possibly carry and stumbled through the sand to the path that led to the car park. And it was like two drowned rats that they eventually and breathlessly slammed themselves into the comfortable front seats of the Range Rover as the storm continued to rage.

'Oh, I'm making puddles all over your seat!' Domenica groaned as she pushed her dripping hair out of her eyes and shivered.

'They'll dry. Here.' He reached across to the back seat and produced a lightweight, zip-front jacket lined with checked flannel. 'All the towels, the blanket, everything else, are soaked.'

'Thanks, but what about you?'

He shrugged. 'It'll warm up—did you say you'd brought some coffee? That's the one thing Mrs Bush didn't think of.'

'Yes! And some carrot cake.' Domenica shrugged into his jacket and twisted around to look over the back of her seat, then knelt up on it. 'I can reach it easier than you may be able to.' Five minutes later she handed him a cup of still-steaming coffee and a piece of carrot cake on a paper plate.

When she had her own coffee and cake, she settled back and said humorously, 'We should have known. It poured yesterday and that stormy, summer heat was really building up!'

He balanced his cup on the dashboard and ate some cake before he said, 'Yes. Listen, I think you should rest your case too, Domenica.'

'Angus—' she hesitated '—I—'

'What I mean is—you're charged with nothing more than I am. It happened because neither of us could help it. But if you don't care to admit anything else, even to yourself, I think you should admit that.'

'All right, I do,' she said after a long pause during which the storm started to abate. 'But there's not much more I want to—think about at this stage.'

He put his arm along the back of her seat and studied her with detached interest. 'Do you want me to come to dinner with your mother Friday week?'

Domenica flinched inwardly because she could sense the change of atmosphere. While the tension might be slackening outside as the storm swept out to sea, tension was gathering and threading the air with pointed little barbs within the Range Rover.

Perhaps she had initiated it, she reflected, but he had come back with a counter-punch that had activated all her old doubts, all her instinctive wariness of this man. And brought all her mother's problems to the fore again.

She looked across at him at last. His dark hair was flattened to his head and hanging in his eyes. The little star-shaped scar at the end of one eyebrow seemed to stand out more, perhaps because he was cold. But his grey eyes were shockingly indifferent as they roamed her still-damp skin and the way her amazing eyelashes were clumped together with droplets of moisture, then it came to rest on her mouth.

I am not going to be steamrollered into bed by this man! She didn't say it but she thought it. I am not going to be swamped by a tidal wave of sensuality although I can't deny it exists between us. I *am* going to get my mother's affairs sorted out before I go any further down this road, Angus Keir. It's the only way I might be able to…get things into a proper perspective….

Then she muttered, 'What the hell?' and said it all word for word.

A weak ray of sunlight lit the interior of the car as she finished speaking.

She blinked, then blinked again because, instead of the cynical disdain she'd been expecting, his eyes had started to dance in that disconcerting way they sometimes had.

'You're not—going to shoot me down in flames?' Her expression was incredulous.

'I always admire a fighter, even when I'm the one on the ropes,' he murmured. 'Don't let it fool you into a false sense of security, however, Domenica. Because I don't intend to give up. So. Dinner with you and your mother on

Friday or not? I can always take her to dinner on her own if you like.'

'No,' she said rapidly, then breathed heavily and could have shot him for the undisguised amusement in his eyes now.

To make matters worse he added, 'If you're really afraid of what I might put her up to, I agree, you'd be better off being there.'

She clenched her teeth. 'All right.'

He reached for the key and started the Range Rover. 'Then let me get you home.' He swung the wheel and drove out of the car park. But he looked at her as he stopped to check the traffic before turning onto the road. 'Was it all a penance today, though?'

'It was,' she swallowed then said with gloomy honesty, 'one of the nicer days I've spent for a while, for the most part.'

'Goodness me,' he murmured, 'I'll pop that under my pillow and dream sweet dreams upon it, Miss Harris.'

'You're impossible,' she said. 'Did you know that?'

'Some women have told me I'm a few things but that hasn't actually featured amongst them,' he reflected gravely.

'Because they may not have had an ounce of backbone between them!' she retorted.

'Perhaps,' he agreed comfortably. 'Just think how good you are for my inflated ego.'

This time Domenica had the sense to withdraw from the contest—in a way.

She said ingenuously, 'Goodness me, who would have thought the weather could be so fine now? That's Sydney for you, though, I guess.'

She had ten days' grace until her mother's dinner after the picnic on the beach.

They'd parted amiably enough, on the surface, after the picnic. He'd made no suggestion that they get together before the dinner and insisted she keep his jacket rather than trail inside looking completely bedraggled. In fact, she'd rather got the impression as he'd helped her out of the car and handed her her belongings that he'd been short of time and had had his mind elsewhere. Not that he hadn't been courteous, but in a brief kind of way.

So be it, she'd thought, and been briefly courteous in return as she'd thanked him, said goodbye and walked indoors without a backward glance.

And she kept hold of that so-be-it frame of mind for the next few days. She refused to be anything other than casual and humorous when Natalie wanted to know how it had gone. Instead of being the slightest bit vague, she worked keenly and industriously and came up with a sports bodysuit design that Natalie was in transports over.

She also parcelled up Angus's jacket and had it delivered to the Keir Conway head office the day after the picnic.

Three days after the picnic, she picked up her mail on her way home from work to find a heavy packet amongst it. There were two books but no note inside, she found, after she'd kicked off her shoes and made herself a cup of tea.

She sat down with them in her comfortable lounge with its parchment walls and cranberry linen-covered suite, wooden louvre blinds and lovely terracotta urns filled with dried leaves and flowers, and her collection of elephants, small and large although not life-size, of course, but wooden, stone and one lovely leather one.

One book was a beautiful and glossy history of fashion design that set her mouth watering as she paged through it.

The other was a novel, obviously read because the pages didn't have that snug crispness of an unread book, although it was still in excellent condition. It was a novel she and Angus Keir had discussed over lunch on the way home from Lidcombe Peace—she to say she was looking forward to reading it but hadn't bought a copy yet; he to say he was halfway through it and enjoying it.

So, despite the absence of any note, she didn't really need to flip the packet over to see a Keir Conway label with a printed return address on it, although she did so anyway. And she stared into space for a good five minutes before she remembered her tea and drank it.

Three days later, a much slimmer packet arrived bearing that same Keir Conway label. A CD this time, and this time there was a note signed Angus, that simply said he thought she might enjoy it. She slipped it into her CD player and was transported straight to the continent of Africa via the most wonderful mixture of jungle and jive music, full of drums and penny whistles, rhythm and tempo. It was fair to say she not only enjoyed it, she loved it.

But what to do about these gifts? The fashion book had inspired her with some new ideas for girls' dresses as well as some different and wonderful combinations of colours. She was finding the novel hard to put down and she was often to be heard whistling and humming the music. So he couldn't have chosen better, she had to acknowledge, which must have involved some thought and some insight into her preferences.

And she found herself wondering what kind of insight she had into Angus Keir's preferences and how she would go about repaying these gifts in kind, if she were prompted to do so. She even found herself staring at a small painting in an art shop near work that was a vibrant depiction of an outback scene of sage-green spinifex on red soil and a drover on horseback. But would those memories be painful? she wondered.

Then she shook herself mentally and decided the problem was not whether to shower him with gifts in return but how, and when, to thank him for his.

Three days before her mother's dinner, an opportunity presented itself but it took her a good ten minutes of hanging on to the phone and explaining to several people who she was to even reach him. Which made her less sure that she was doing the right thing, and less able to sound relaxed.

But he himself was slightly clipped when she finally got him.

'Domenica?'

'Yes, Angus. I'm sorry to bother you but—'

'Don't be,' he interrupted. 'I should have thought to give you a direct number but I am slightly tied up at the moment.'

'Oh. Well…' she could hear how cool she sounded but was unable to do a thing to rectify it '...I'll be brief. Thank you very much for the books and CD. I...I loved them. But the other reason I'm ringing is because I've had an offer for the Blacktown site. It's a bit less than you suggested but—'

'Then don't take it.' He was absolutely decisive.

Domenica drew a breath and said politely, 'If you'd let me finish, yes, it is lower...' she told him how much '...but they're offering a significant deposit, a thirty-day settlement and no subject-to-finance clause, so...' She paused.

'Which they're hoping will seduce you into accepting less than what it's worth, Domenica. Go back to them with my figure and not a penny less.'

'I...I don't know if I have the nerve,' she said, sounding absolutely genuine for the first time in their conversation. 'It's like throwing away a bird in the hand for two in the bush!'

'Why don't you think of how many new dresses and how much French champagne the difference could buy your mother?' he recommended, sounding amused.

'Angus,' she said a little desperately, 'are you sure they'll...?' She broke off helplessly.

'If they don't, someone else will. Now's the time to exercise your backbone, Domenica, although, of course, it's entirely up to you. Look, I am sorry, I have to go but I'll see you on Friday night.'

The phone went dead and Domenica took it from her ear to stare at it furiously. And not only on account of being hung up on but the way he'd turned her own words against her, words like backbone and seduce.

Then Friday was upon her, her nerves were in tatters and she arrived at Rose Bay to discover that her mother had prepared a minor banquet. There was to be a pork crackling and potato salad on a bed of frisée lettuce to start, a rack of lamb with a mustard and herb stuffing accompanied by honeyed carrots and hot, fresh asparagus, and a berry jelly—a symphony of strawberries, raspberries and blueberries in a clear jelly mould garnished with cream—for dessert.

The Sèvres dinner service was on display on an exquisite heavy lace tablecloth and the

Stuart crystal was out. Candles stood ready in the Georgian silver candlesticks and some perfect camellia blooms floated in a bowl between them.

Her first reaction was sheer exasperation. Her mother was in fact an excellent cook and had passed it on to her, although Christy had missed out on the cooking gene altogether. Which meant she wouldn't have been of much help. Nor, since the decline of the family fortunes, did Barbara have the kind of domestic help she was used to and had been used to all her life. So, while preparing delectable dishes might come naturally to her, clearing up, polishing the silver and crystal and all the rest did not. And it was plain to see that she looked tired and overwrought.

Then guilt superseded Domenica's exasperation and she thanked heaven that she'd come early.

'Looks lovely and smells delicious!' she said as she kissed her mother and hugged her. 'Why don't you go and have a nice soak in the bath? I'll do the rest. You've got plenty of time—I'll bring you a glass of champagne while you're dressing!' It had been a custom of her father's, and for an instant she saw a sparkle of tears in her mother's eyes. So she hugged her again and held her until the threat of tears had subsided. 'Off you go,' she said softly. 'I'm sure you're going to look a million dollars tonight!'

The candles had burnt halfway down, liqueurs and coffee were on the table before any mention of business was made. And then it was Barbara who brought it up, perhaps emboldened by a successful dinner party.

It had been successful although there were only the four of them, Angus Keir reflected. The food had been delicious with the serving of most of it discreetly managed by Domenica, wearing a silky wheat-coloured, cowl-neck camisole and slim black trousers. Her dark hair was up tonight in a smooth pleat and several gold chains circled the fine smooth skin of her neck. He'd noticed immediately that she was wearing black sandals with slim, high heels.

Christy had opted for a chalk-blue straight sleeveless linen dress with tiny metallic motifs embroidered over it and Barbara was elegant in a slim wattle-yellow suit. Not only good-looking and elegant were the Harris women, he mused as he toyed with his coffee spoon, but good company, skilled at drawing people out, and their inter-family repartee had been natural and funny.

But he couldn't help wondering if it was his imagination or whether Domenica had a look of strain in her beautiful blue eyes from time to time, and faint shadows beneath them. And whether the lovely lines and curves of her body beneath the silky top and slim trousers were a little taut. Nor could he dispel the impression that without her managerial skills this dinner party might have been a disaster. And it was already obvious, he reminded himself, that she bore the real burden of Barbara's problems.

So when Barbara said, 'Angus, we normally retire to the lounge for coffee but would you mind if we sat here to discuss—things?' he said that, smiling warmly at her, no, he wouldn't mind at all, and drew some sheets of paper from the pocket of his navy-blue suit.

'I made a few notes,' he went on. 'Some suggestions that might help—they mostly hinge on the sale of Blacktown, but perhaps not the most significant one.' He glanced at Domenica.

She cleared her throat. 'I did as you suggested with the Blacktown offer, although I also consulted Mum and Christy. I haven't heard back yet. May I see your suggestions?'

He passed the papers across the table. She studied it intently but looked up only moments later. 'No. Uh—sorry, I forgot to tell you but...' She paused and glanced at her mother, and seemed lost for words.

'What is it?' Barbara enquired.

'Well, we were hoping to keep this house for you—'

'It's entirely impractical,' Angus said.

They all stared at him wordlessly. In his navy suit, pale blue shirt and diagonally striped blue and grey tie, he looked not only impeccably tailored and groomed but there was an aura of quiet authority about him.

'The rates alone are prohibitive,' he went on. 'Maintenance on a house of this age and size is another drain and just the normal up-keep of it domestically and garden-wise is terribly expensive.' He stopped at a slight sound from Barbara.

Then he continued with the same unemphatic but steady assurance, 'Whereas, Barbara, if you disposed of this house as well as Blacktown, that would not only completely clear the backlog of debt, but, if you invested wisely, you could afford something smaller although still pleasant and with harbour views, you could have a decent income to rely on for the rest of your life, you would not be left alone in a huge house should Christy get married, for example, and you could afford to indulge yourself now and then.'

The stricken expression on Barbara Harris's face, which had made Domenica curve her hands into fists beneath the table and send Angus a killing little look, changed slowly. 'How?' she asked.

'You might like to take a cruise once in a while, you might like to spend a spring in Paris or a summer in Tuscany. Perhaps there are some music festivals around the world you'd like to attend, or wouldn't it be nice to be able to hold your own musical soirées without wondering if you're going to break the bank?'

He paused and looked around. 'You have such exquisite taste you might even like to start dealing in antiques or paintings.' His gaze came to rest on her face again. 'I know you've been a widow for eighteen months now, Barbara,' he added gently, 'but I'm sure your husband would rest happier to know you can go on and live comfortably, doing the things you love.'

Barbara Harris took a deep breath and looked around. 'You're right,' she said tremulously. 'He isn't here in these bricks and mortar although that's why I didn't want to sell. He's in my heart and he always will be. I'll do it.'

'I don't *believe* it,' Domenica said as she and Angus stood at the gate not much later. She rubbed her face wearily. 'I always knew it was what she should do but every time I brought the subject up she got so distressed! And I thought you believed you'd be able to save this place for her?'

'That was before I met her and had a chance to think about what the real reason she might be clinging onto it was,' he replied. 'Also, sometimes there's a time and place for things. I just happened to get lucky and pick the right time tonight. Something else is worrying you, though?'

She half smiled. They were standing beneath a street light and for the first time she noticed a couple of silver strands in his hair. 'No, not really, well...' She trailed off. Then she straightened her shoulders. 'Could I make you dinner tomorrow night, Angus? Or—'

He looked down at her in the unsmiling way she now knew. And responded formally, 'Thank you very much, that's very kind of you. But I'm moving into Lidcombe Peace tomorrow.'

'Of course—I'd forgotten.'

'You could come down for a day, though,' he said. 'I'll be there all weekend—all week, come to that—and there are a few things I'd like to show you.' He shrugged. 'No need to call, just turn up. If you're so minded, Domenica,' he added.

'I...'

'I'd also recommend that you get a good night's sleep.' He pulled a hand from his trouser pocket and touched her chin lightly with his knuckles. 'You look as if you could do with it, mate,' he added quizzically.

A couple of moments later, she watched the Range Rover drive away. But it was a few minutes more before she returned to her mother's house, where she was going to spend the night.

All through the next morning, Saturday, Domenica was amazed by the difference in her mother. It was almost as if she'd been reborn a calmer and more mature person. It was obvious that not only had she come to grips with life without Walter Harris, but she had a purpose now. She even compiled a list of what she would take with her from Rose Bay and what she would sell—with a surprisingly realistic grasp of values. And the three of them discussed where she'd like to move to.

Then, around lunch-time, Domenica got a call on her mobile phone from the real estate agent she was dealing with, saying that he had a signed offer in his hand for the Blacktown property at Angus's valuation and still the same conditions: a thirty-day settlement, a significant deposit and no subject-to-finance clause.

'So he was right,' Christy said, a little awe-struck.

The relief Domenica felt was tremendous. Until, that was, she got home to her apartment later in the day. To find that one burden had been replaced by another. She was deeply in Angus Keir's debt. But not only for his financial advice, for something else. For taking the time to understand her mother and exercise an *invaluable* influence over her.

The only problem was, if she wished to repay him in any way it was to be on his terms or nothing, she had the distinct feeling. Go down to Lidcombe Peace this weekend, for example. What would be the consequence of not going down to Lidcombe Peace? she wondered. To be thought of as still seeing herself too good for him?

And she was the one who had flung down the gauntlet, another one, she thought dismally, of not being willing to go down any road with him until her mother's life was sorted out. Well, it was now, but she still had that residue of wariness towards Angus Keir, that *something* that was holding her back from what she knew would be the inevitable outcome of getting to know him better.

Still, she thought, it would be churlish not to make some attempt to thank him and what harm could spending a few hours down at Lidcombe tomorrow do? No, it was more than that, she realized. It was a matter of pride. She couldn't in all conscience ignore him or wait for him to make the next move.

There was another car on the gravel roundabout in front of Lidcombe Peace when she arrived at about eleven the next morning, not Angus's. And as she drew up a party of people came round the corner of the house. Angus, a man and a woman of about the same age, and three children. It was a clear, sparkling day and you could see Sydney in the blue distance.

But she hesitated briefly before opening her door with something of a dilemma on her mind. Strangers, or other people, might help— or they might not. If they knew him well, it might be the cause of some speculation amongst his circle of friends. Then it struck her that she'd somehow assumed he was a solitary man without thinking much about it at all.

But the one thing she knew, there was no turning back. So she got out of the car in her long beige linen overall dress, worn over a white T-shirt and with black mules, and one of the children, the only girl of about ten years old, rushed up to her and said, 'Wow! You look wonderful. Mum—' she looked over her shoulder '—why can't I have a dress like this?'

It made everyone laugh and Angus came forward to make the introductions. But it turned out that his friends, Peter and Lorraine Bailey, having spent the morning at Lidcombe Peace, were on the point of leaving.

'We were dying to see it!' Lorraine Bailey confided to Domenica. 'And we've made Angus promise to have a housewarming party! But we've got a school fête on today so we ought to get going.'

And they finally wrestled their three reluctant children into the car and drove off waving.

Angus dropped his hand and looked down at Domenica. 'You came. You also conquered, and not only Madeleine,' he said with a smile lurking at the back of his eyes.

Domenica shrugged. 'Only because of a dress—'

'Not only because of a dress,' he contradicted, and said no more, but his grey gaze skimmed down her figure, then came back to rest on her loose hair that a gentle breeze was lifting, and the contours of her face.

'Well, I came,' Domenica said, controlling the tremor that ran through her, 'with a set plan in mind.'

He raised an eyebrow at her.

'Yes.' She walked to the hatchback of her car and opened it to lift out a basket covered with a checked cloth. 'I came to make you lunch. A very special lunch, as it happens.'

'You didn't have to do that, Domenica.'

'I felt like it,' she responded demurely.

'Some sort of culinary masterpiece?' he hazarded.

'Oh, definitely. Hamburgers. And I brought some beer just in case you didn't have any in stock.'

She stopped as he started to laugh, then he took the basket from her and said, 'You're a genius, Miss Harris. I would kill for a hamburger and a beer right now.'

He sat at the kitchen table while Domenica moved around it and displayed her familiarity with the kitchen as she cooked the hamburgers she'd pre-prepared, warmed the rolls and chopped salad to go with them.

'Does this give you a sense of *déjà vu*?' he asked at one point.

She waved the spatula over a couple of eggs she was frying. 'I guess so, but I'm also intensely grateful to you, Angus. All of a sudden my life seems so much less complicated now and my mother is like a new person.' She looked over her shoulder at him briefly and started to tell him about the Blacktown news too.

He listened in silence and said nothing when she'd finished speaking until, at last, she had to turn to him again. 'I had to say it, I am very grateful,' she said helplessly.

He'd opened a bottle of beer and he swung it idly by the neck between two fingers as he regarded her steadily. He wore a khaki bush shirt stained with sweat, with jeans and short boots, his hair was ruffled and there were blue shadows on his jaw. 'So long as it's not the only reason you came here today, Domenica.'

She turned back to the eggs and lifted them carefully out to set them on top of the burgers. 'There. All done. Would you mind getting me a tray—out of that cupboard?' She pointed. 'And why don't we eat outside?'

'Domenica.' He didn't move.

She rested half a bun on top of each deluxe hamburger with all the trimmings—eggs, pine-apple, bacon and salad—and piled the chips she'd also made beside them.

Then she turned and leant back against the counter, and their gazes clashed. 'Something still makes me—wary of you, Angus. I don't know what it is but it's there. So I'm not sure…why else I came. I do know I had to thank you, though. Nor did I get a chance to thank you properly for the books and CD. You couldn't have chosen better.'

'You don't think you're tilting at windmills?'

She shrugged and crossed her arms over her waist. 'I don't know. I would like to think…I can be sensible and take heed of my intuition, that's all.'

He smiled briefly. 'My intuition tells me you don't like to surrender the lead, Domenica, but let's not let your culinary masterpiece get cold.' He got up at last and produced the tray.

'Tell me about the Baileys?' she invited as they ate outside with the breeze wafting the scent of roses over them, and an awkward sense of constraint between them, at least on her part.

'I met Pete years ago when I was at night school studying economics. He was doing law. And, although he didn't come from quite as far west as Tibooburra, we had that in common. We've been friends ever since. I was his best man when he married Lorraine and I'm Darcy's godfather. Darcy is the elder boy. Pete has a thriving law practice now and Lorraine is an ardent florist with her own business.'

'I liked them.'

He glanced at her. 'So do I.'

'Do you have many friends like that?' Domenica asked as she finished her lunch and patted her stomach ruefully.

'A few. And quite a few unlike that. Did you imagine me as being completely self-contained?' The look in his grey eyes was faintly sardonic.

'It's not hard to imagine you as a kind of Lone Ranger, Angus,' she retaliated without thinking.

'And Lorraine and Pete didn't reassure you that I'm really quite normal?' he countered dryly.

She stood up.

'So now you're about to run back to town?' he speculated, sprawling back in the teak garden chair. 'Because you've done your duty, paid your debt—as you see it?'

'I always knew it would come down to that,' she said tautly.

'No, you didn't,' he drawled, then stood up himself. 'It's a convenient excuse you devised because you're scared of letting yourself go, Domenica, for one of two reasons. You like to see yourself as the boss at all times or—you really do think you're too good for me.'

He paused as she stiffened, then went on, 'But, believe me, my dear, I prefer my encounters with women to be of the mutually satisfactory variety, and if you are that stuck-up, then why *don't* you run back to town?' he finished lethally.

She did just that. She stalked to her car, got in and drove away as far as the gate which was about half a mile from the house. She was so angry she nearly ran over a Hereford cow on the way but it was that that stopped her. Not so much the shock of it, although she did get a fright—but the fact that it was there. And she looked back to see some more Hereford cattle grazing in the paddock beside the drive, splendid animals that would have brought tears of joy to her Lidcombe grandmother's eyes.

She also saw that a new race and loading yard had been built and new fences erected and she remembered on Friday night Angus saying that he had some things to show her and her heart jolted for some reason.

She stopped just before the gate and dropped her head into her hands. Then she turned the car around and drove back.

He was still outside but sitting again at the teak garden setting around the other side of the house, with his feet up on a bench. He had his back to her but she could see a fresh bottle of beer in his hand. And he was staring out over his kingdom but not in a way that was relaxed or as if it gave him much pleasure.

She saw the already tense line of his shoulders tense further as she said quietly, 'I do tend to be bossy, I can give off the impression that I'm stuck-up, but no man has made me feel the way you do, Angus, and I'm not sure how to handle it. If you'd like to take the time to help me—handle it, if you'd like to show me your improvements of Lidcombe Peace along the way, I...would like that.'

He didn't move for a long moment, and she felt her heart start to sink. Then he stood up carefully, put the beer down and turned to her, and said nothing. But he put out his hand to her, and after she'd taken it and they'd stared into each other's eyes for a long time he drew her into his arms and said her name into her hair in that same, slightly unsteady way she remembered from the beach.

CHAPTER FOUR

'RIGHT, enough of this,' he said a little later.

'I have to agree,' she responded but made no move to leave the circle of his arms. Instead she put the tip of her finger to the scar at the end of his eyebrow. 'How did that come about?'

'I fell off a horse into a barbed wire fence.'

'Ouch! You're lucky you didn't lose an eye.'

'Mmm... Talking of eyes, yours are the most amazing. And with your hair loose like this, you remind me of a gorgeous, blue-eyed gypsy girl.' He twined his fingers through it.

'First a mermaid, now a gypsy,' she teased.

'Both capable of seriously interfering with my equilibrium. The fact that I don't seem to be able to let you go should testify to that.'

She laughed and leant against him. 'I have not the slightest inclination to be released, as it happens, so you may as well kiss me again,

Angus Keir. Then we might be able to get on and do…other things!'

He stared down into her eyes a little narrowly.

'Or—' she looked wry '—would that be putting too much pressure on—us?'

He started to say something but she got the impression it wasn't his first choice of words that emerged. He said, 'I could kiss you until the cows come home, Domenica, so, no, it would be my pleasure.' And he started to do so.

But when he'd done with her—why did she think of it like that? she wondered—she knew that her light-hearted words about pressure had turned back to haunt her if not to say taunt her. Because what started out as playful and curiously friendly became again that leaping flame between them. Had she expected a repeat of their first kiss when she'd come back to find him on the veranda? But that had been more a mental union, she now realized. An unspoken relief that they'd found some accord, a quiet, although deep gratitude that they were together.

But as he moulded her body to his and she responded with her arms around him, as he kissed her mouth, then her throat and his thumbs found her nipples unerringly, even beneath her clothes they flowered and she not only felt like a seductive siren or a tempting, blue-eye gypsy girl, she was swept with joyful rapture.

And she kissed him ardently in return. She slid her arms around his neck and made no protest when his hands found their way below her overall dress and beneath her T-shirt to circle her slim, bare waist then wander down towards her hips, she revelled in the sensations he aroused and let her own hands explore the feel of his skin and his shoulders beneath the khaki shirt.

The rough and the smooth, the thought chased through her mind. The slight abrasion of those blue shadows on his jaw against her cheek, but the sleek skin and powerful muscles of his shoulders under her fingers. The sheer temptation—was another thought that skipped through her mind—of a man who could handle her in a way that made her feel glorious. The allure of the tanned column of his throat beneath her lips, the friction of her breasts against his chest, and the little glint of passion in the smoky-grey of his eyes beneath heavy lids, when he made her gasp with pleasure and arch her body even closer against him.

But how to cope, when it ended, with a feeling of loss and incompleteness? How to be unaware that she was hectically flushed and trembling, dishevelled and not quite steady on her feet—unaware that her mouth felt bruised and there was an ache within her, of frustration.

'I see what you mean,' she managed to murmur finally as she combed her fingers through her hair, pulled her T-shirt down beneath her dress and licked her lips several times.

He took her hands and stilled them between his. 'What?'

She shrugged. 'Well, you didn't say it, I did, but it was a thoughtless thing to say.'

He narrowed his eyes. 'About pressure?'

'Didn't you—' she paused briefly '—just show me that I was playing with fire, Angus?'

'If so,' he said steadily, but she noticed a nerve beating in his jaw, 'there can be no flame without a match. But let's not get too technical.' A smile started at the back of his eyes. 'Instead of me kissing you until the cows come home, Domenica, may I show you my cows instead?'

It took a moment for her to rearrange her mind set. *Had* she been warned? Against lighting a flame that could become a bush fire? Or not? she wondered, then shook her head slightly. 'Uh, you may. I nearly ran one over earlier—it's OK, I missed it.'

They did a tour of the whole property by foot and Range Rover. He told her all his plans and she was able to contribute with things she remembered from the past. Where there had been fence lines and paddocks, how the bottom of one paddock tended to flood, where frost had wiped out a crop her father had experimented with, and the exact spot she'd fallen into the creek that meandered through the property, aged four.

'I got a belting for it,' she reminisced with her mouth curving. 'I couldn't swim then and they got the fright of their lives before they could fish me out. I was trying to catch a fish and, although it was only about three feet deep, it was running quite strongly. I ended up over there.' She pointed to some slippery rocks. 'All torn, muddy and coughing up water.'

He laughed. 'That might have been punishment enough.'

'I wasn't supposed to be anywhere near the creek, let alone fishing in it.'

He raised an eyebrow at her. 'So you were an adventurous kid?'

'I suspect I was a right handful but perhaps more in my teenage years,' she confessed after a moment's thought. 'How about you?'

'I suspect the same, if the number of beltings I got were any indication. Although I can remember the day my father suddenly realized I might be more than a match for him.'

They were sitting on a grassy peak beside the Range Rover, overlooking most of the property, and he was chewing a stalk of grass.

'Did you like him?' Domenica asked abruptly. 'Is he still alive?'

'No. And no.'

'Not even now, with the vision of hind-sight?'

'No. I tried to believe he was the kind of man he was because of my mother's desertion, whatever the whys and wherefores of that, and, yes, it hardened him even more but—there was nothing I could have done about it.'

'No,' she said slowly. 'Was it a very hard upbringing?'

He shrugged. 'There was a lot to recommend it, actually. If you like open spaces, physical activity, horses, pitting yourself against the elements, flood but mostly drought, et cetera, if you measure your achievements in those terms and have an affinity with the land and the mysticism of the real outback, it can be bewitching. I felt all those things,' he said reflectively, 'but I knew I needed more.'

She watched him as he stared out over the very different, green and fertile acres of Lidcombe Peace, fascinated by his eloquence and the mental images he'd conjured. And she said at last, 'This must seem like a—toy environment in contrast, though.'

He glanced at her. 'Perhaps. But I've built a company, I own...other bricks and mortar, as your mother put it, but these are the first acres I've ever owned and can do what I like with.'

It amazed Domenica how his words moved her.

Then he said quietly, 'Will you stay the night? In your own bed and your own room?'

She looked away and studied the cloud shadows on the pasture and the dark green lines of the huge old hoop pine trees an ancestor of hers had planted, and knew she'd like nothing better than to stay but wondered if she'd have the strength of mind to do so on a platonic basis.

'Would you hold it against me if I did stay—in my own bed and my own room? In view of how we affect each other?' she asked straightly.

'Domenica...' he said her name as if the cadences of it were especially intriguing to him at the moment '...no, I wouldn't. I'd be too happy to have your company to hold anything against you. But if I do get any foolish ideas, you may slap me down smartly.'

'It's myself I'm a little worried about,' she said ruefully, 'and don't you dare laugh at me, Angus Keir!'

But he did, and she laughed with him as he hugged her then put her away from him with decision. And they got up and drove back to the house.

'That's called—letting your fingers do the walking,' Domenica said rather sternly.

They were sitting in the lounge on a thick rug, leaning back against a heavy settee and watching the flames of a blaze Angus had lit in the fireplace to counteract the chill of the higher air of the Razorback Range, as well as a day that had clouded over towards the end of it. A bottle of wine stood in a cooler on the low table beside them. She had her glass in her hands but he didn't appear to be interested in his wine.

He had his arm round her shoulders and his long fingers were caressing the side of her neck, a light pattern that was nevertheless interfering with her breathing.

'These fingers would love to walk all over you, Domenica, but they shall desist. Shortly,' he said.

'Good. Because dinner will be ready shortly.'

'Yes, ma'am. Can I do anything?'

'You could set the table.' She put her wine down, stretched and levered herself up. Then she laughed down at his expression. 'It was either that or—let dinner burn,' she said.

'I know what you mean,' he replied gravely. 'I'll bring the wine.'

She'd found his fridge well stocked but she'd made a simple meal of macaroni cheese and a salad. And as they ate she asked him if he intended to 'do' for himself, and why, as she looked around, could she see nothing that hadn't always been at Lidcombe Peace?

'Because all my things are still packed in boxes sitting in the garage,' he answered. 'And Mrs Bush is coming down tomorrow for a few days to do the unpacking as well as attend to hiring some local help for me.'

'So you're not moving the invaluable Mrs Bush down here permanently? Incidentally, I can give her a few names.'

'Thank you. And no, I'll still be spending time in town so I need her there. Besides which, she doesn't like the country.'

'Where—how do you live in town?' Domenica asked curiously, then gestured. 'I mean, in a house, an apartment, on the harbour or…?'

'On the harbour, on the north shore, in a penthouse with lovely views of the water.'

'How nice.'

'It is.' He looked at her quizzically. 'How about your apartment?'

'It has one bedroom, it overlooks a park but has no harbour views.' She stopped and looked around suddenly at the lovely interior of Lidcombe Peace.

'It's not exactly in enemy hands, Domenica,' he said quietly.

'No.' She pushed her hair back behind her ears. 'No, of course not.'

'Has it suddenly hit you that it's gone, in a manner of speaking?'

'It's suddenly hit me that I feel...a little unreal,' she said slowly. 'And a little rootless. My father always used to sit where you're sitting, for example. We always used to have macaroni cheese for dinner on Sunday nights when we were here—I didn't even realize while I was doing it that it was sheer habit.'

He watched her for a long moment, then he stood up and came round to help her up. And he drew her by the hand into the lounge, sat her down in a comfortable armchair and pulled a footstool up for her. He threw another log onto the fire and put a CD onto the stereo that was built into the wall. 'I did unpack my music,' he said with a glimmer of a smile, and poured her the last of the wine. 'Relax. I'll make the coffee.'

It was Mendelssohn that flooded the room, 'A Midsummer Night's Dream', and she sighed with pleasure and sank back with her eyes closed.

Presently, she opened them at a sound to see him standing in front of her with a tray and blushed, because she'd been conducting the 'Wedding March' vigorously with her hands.

'You do like your music,' he said, putting the tray on the table and sitting down on the edge of the footstool.

She moved her feet so he had more room. 'Yes. But so do you, I gather. That African CD was wonderful. I got some of the tunes on the brain!'

He laughed and poured the coffee out of a percolator. Then he opened a bottle of cognac and tipped a dram into each cup.

Domenica widened her eyes but accepted her cup. 'Do I look as if I need a little... fortification out of a bottle?'

'You look better,' he observed. 'Less haunted.'

She grimaced and sipped her coffee.

'You've been the strong one for a long time, I would imagine,' he suggested. 'It's only natural for a reaction to set in.'

'Perhaps.' She laid her head back.

'How's business?' he asked after a pause.

'Blooming. I've sold the design for an aerobics bodysuit to a chain of upmarket sportswear shops. We go into production in a week.' She lifted her head. 'I'm hiring more machinists and cutters.' She stopped and sat up, suddenly struck. 'I really will have to leave at the crack of dawn tomorrow! I've got interviews starting at nine o'clock.'

'That's OK,' he said easily. 'I'll be spending Friday night in town. There's a Mozart by Moonlight concert in the Botanic Gardens. Would you like to come?'

'Is that all you're going back for?' she asked a little surprisedly.

'No. That and business.' He raised an eyebrow at her.

'I'd love to come.'

'I'll pick you up, it starts at eight so—'

'Come to dinner about six,' she interrupted. 'That'll give us plenty of time.' She yawned suddenly and eyed her coffee-cup comically.

'Time for bed,' he said, standing up. 'Can I lend you a T-shirt?'

She got up and looked around. 'There it is, no, thanks, I'll use this.' She picked up her beautiful mocha pashmina wrap that she'd brought in from her car earlier, and without which she rarely left home.

'A scarf?' he said quizzically.

'Not a scarf, not a shawl, a wrap and not any old wrap either,' she contradicted. 'A pashmina wrap and just about the most useful and lovely part of my wardrobe.' She ran its silken softness through her fingers, then shook it open to its full extent.

'What is pashmina?' he asked.

'The finest, lightest, softest cashmere,' she explained. 'This one in particular is seventy per cent cashmere and thirty per cent silk. All the most elegant women possess a pashmina these days,' she added with an impish glint in her eyes.

'I see. I'm still not quite sure how you'll wear it—to bed.'

'As a sarong.' She shook it again and wound it around her. 'Like so.'

He said nothing but when she looked up from the pashmina into his eyes, it was to see they were arrested in a way that left her in no doubt he was visualizing her wearing nothing but the wrap.

She unwound it and bunched it up in her hands. 'Sorry. That was thoughtless, again,' she said unevenly, with colour fluctuating in her cheeks and an inner trembling taking possession of her as she was drawn into a circle of physical awareness.

He still said nothing but it was impossible to be oblivious to the sensuous pull between them—the air was charged with it. The way his dark hair fell, the lines of his face, the scar on his eyebrow, the magnificence of his beautifully co-ordinated body even so still as it was now, the memory of his hands on her—all these things spoke to her senses and drew a response that made her breathe raggedly and yearn physically for his touch and the sheer fire power of what they did to each other.

It also gave her an intimation that, even closed into her own bedroom and own bed, there would be little relief from the urgency of these sensations.

She opened her hands in a helpless little gesture and the pashmina dropped to the floor.

He ignored it and spoke at last, his grey eyes ranging from her hair to her mouth, to her breasts. 'We can do it, Domenica, so long as you don't regret it in the morning.'

She bent down to retrieve her wrap and asked the only question she could think of as she straightened, 'How can I know...that?'

He smiled, but not with his eyes. 'If you can't, let's wait until you're—clearer in your mind about it. Goodnight, my dear.' He waited, then when she didn't respond, although she looked supremely disconsolate and confused, he did smile genuinely. And he stepped forward to kiss her lightly on the lips. 'Go to bed. It's not the end of the world. Just cold-shower time!'

On Thursday evening he rang her at home to tell her he wouldn't be able to make dinner with her the following evening but if she could put herself in a taxi and get to the Botanic Gardens, could he meet her there?

'I—yes, why not?' she said down the phone, hoping her disappointment didn't make itself heard in her voice.

'I'm sorry about this,' he said.

She gritted her teeth—he had heard it.

'But,' he continued, 'I have to leave for Singapore at the crack of dawn on Saturday morning—something has come up out of the blue and I've got wall-to-wall appointments until about seven tomorrow.'

'That's OK,' she said brightly. 'Shall I meet you on the harbour wall?' She named a spot.

'Yes. Perhaps we could turn dinner at your apartment into supper, after the concert?'

'All right. See you!' She put the phone down, and sat down to think.

She'd left Lidcombe Peace in a rush on Monday morning, having only slept fitfully then, towards dawn, so deeply, it had taken Angus several raps on her door to wake her.

She'd showered hastily and emerged to find that he'd made breakfast: bacon, eggs, toast and a pot of strong tea. She'd also winced visibly at the impact of him, shaved, clear-eyed and as invigorated-looking as only someone who'd been out and about in the brisk, early morning air could.

Whereas she'd had faint shadows under her eyes, no make-up, nothing even to tie her hair back with, and yesterday's clothes on.

That it had all coloured her mood, that she was jittery at the prospect of dashing back to town had, apparently, amused him.

And she'd told him, as she'd sipped the tea gratefully but contemplated the bacon and eggs rather darkly, that she'd rather he said nothing.

'OK. I take it you're not a morning person, Domenica?' His grey eyes glinted.

'You take it wrong,' she replied gloomily. 'I can be as bright and bouncy as the best of them, but not today.'

'Why don't you eat something?' he suggested.

'Because I feel sick just to think of bacon and eggs—my digestive system has not awoken properly yet.'

He laughed outright and pulled her plate towards him. 'Try the toast with some honey,' he advised, and started to eat her breakfast.

She stared at him. 'Is that your second breakfast or…?'

'My second,' he agreed complacently. 'I've got a lot to do today and I can't stand waste.'

'Now I feel really terrible. You're not only bright and bouncy, sexy and good-looking, you

not only kept me awake in my wretched pashmina for a lot of the night but you're the kind
of ''waste not, want not'' person who will eat
two breakfasts. It's too much!'

'Domenica...' he was still laughing as he
put his knife and fork down '...which would
you prefer? That I throw your breakfast in the
bin or—kiss you until you feel better about
things?'

Her lips curved into a half-smile and she
started to butter a piece of toast. 'I
think...you'd better finish my breakfast.' She
reached for the honey. 'Because in five
minutes I have to be gone.'

She came back to the present and looked
around. She'd taken the call in her bedroom
with its dusky pink walls and carpet, rich raspberry spread on the double bed and sumptuous
pile of pillows in floral pillow cases, pink,
white, raspberry and cornflower blue. The bed
head, side-tables and dressing table were
lovely mahogany antiques brought from
Lidcombe Peace, as it happened, as were some
of the paintings on the walls and the cheval-

mirror that stood in one corner and doubled as a hatstand.

And there always reposed on one bedside table amongst the overflowing books, a sketch-pad and tub of pencils because sitting on her bed against the piled pillows was often where inspiration came to her.

And she found herself rubbing her arms—just as he had done, she recalled, in the moments before they'd parted on Monday. Then he'd taken her hands in his, rested his forehead on hers, and said softly, 'Drive carefully.' And he'd released her, then put into her hands a perfect creamy Peace rosebud.

Emotion had clogged her throat and tears had suddenly threatened although she'd managed to hold them at bay—until she'd been in the car and driving away. Then a couple had slid down her cheeks and splashed onto the bib of her overall dress. But why tears? she wondered now as she'd wondered then. How could he move her so powerfully just by being nice? There was an answer to this of course, she told herself. But was she ready to admit that she was falling more and more in love with Angus Keir?

The next evening, a perfect evening, she sat on the harbour wall not far from the Opera House waiting for him. Although it was a quarter to eight, there was still daylight, a dusky blue version of it that spread over the water and land, softening outlines and gracing the end of a hot day with a cool, filmy bloom.

She wore a long, straight black skirt and a charcoal shirt with the sleeves rolled up to her elbows. Her lips were painted scarlet, the only point of colour about her apart from her eyes, her hair was loose, ruffled and long and she had flat black boots on. But the black and charcoal emphasized the radiance of her pale skin, and the style of shirt and skirt showed off the slenderness of her figure.

There were people about, heading for the concert, but as the minutes ticked by, and he didn't come, the stream of people dried up and she felt unusually alone and isolated. Then he was there, and she swallowed not only in relief, but because he stopped a few paces from her, and it started to happen to her all over again as they stared at each other wordlessly for a long, long moment.

The entrapment of his mere presence in khaki twill trousers, a blue shirt and a checked sports jacket. The mesmerizing of her senses beneath the impact of his height, subdued strength and the way those grey eyes roamed over her.

Then he moved to her and put a hand out to stroke the outline of her face with his fingers. She closed her eyes and turned her lips to kiss his palm, and rested her head against his waist. They stayed like that for a minute or more and it was as if all had been said between them, and all that had been said paled into insignificance beside this physical and mental closeness.

It was still with them when they walked back to his Range Rover after the concert, arm in arm, not only under the spell of Mozart by moonlight, but the spell of their togetherness.

They said little on the way to her apartment and were barely inside the front door when they moved into each other's arms. And it started out as a deep, searching kiss they exchanged, a celebration of their togetherness. But it changed subtly to something that was intoxicating, heady and devastatingly sensual. It became a celebration of their bodies and what they did to each other on a physical plane.

It was mirrored in his indrawn breath when he unbuttoned her charcoal shirt and slid it off her shoulders to reveal a lacy black bra cupping her breasts into twin, creamy with the sheen of satin mounds. And it was in the way he slid his long hands from her narrow waist up beneath her arms and she tilted her head back in sheer pleasure and an unmistakable invitation for him to touch her as he liked.

And when he said, later, with an effort, 'You know where this is leading, Domenica?' she didn't answer in the spoken word, but took his hand and led him into her bedroom.

Where he completed undressing her and picked her up in his arms to lay her on the bed. By the time he joined her, she was shivering—not from cold but reaction to the passion they'd unleashed. The utter absorption in each other, the amazing degree of arousal such as she'd never known; the glorious tangle of their limbs and bodies.

But he quietened her in his arms first, smoothing not only her body with his hands, but her mind with the way he said her name and kissed her lightly but lingeringly until she calmed down. Only then did he begin again to pay attention to the zones on her body that were most vulnerable and only persisting when she bestowed the same attentions upon him so that it was a two-way street of mounting desire. Desire that became a mutual symphony between them during which she gloried in the hard lines of his body, his strength and his gentleness and the pleasure he found in hers, not to mention the pleasure he gave her.

But the crescendo took her breath away as that throbbing pleasure exploded leaving her exposed and racked with delight, completely at his mercy, with only being held hard and feeling the same response in him to sustain her.

They ate supper at two o'clock in the morning. Angus was dressed but she wore a vanilla silk robe over a matching nightgown, and a slightly dazed look in her eyes.

She'd made chicken kebabs with sweet and sour onions and a *panzanella*, a Tuscan bread salad with tuna, anchovies and hard-boiled eggs added to tomatoes, cucumber, chilli and seasoned with black pepper, wine vinegar, oil and basil.

Also capsicum, celery, garlic, sea salt and a day-old baguette, she reminded herself as she tried to eat but could only concentrate, foolishly, on the ingredients of her salad. She'd opened a bottle of claret and it crossed her mind that she'd never needed a full-bodied wine more than she did now. But what to say? How to cope with the aftermath of a lovemaking so powerful, she wasn't sure if she'd ever be the same again?

She'd showered first and come out to set out their supper on her dining-room table while he'd occupied the bathroom but she'd been clumsy and preoccupied—she still was and she felt the silence between them begin to stretch.

Then he said, 'May I?'

She looked at him warily through her lashes.

He stood up and removed their plates to the low table in front of her cranberry settee. Then he came back, picked her up and put her on the settee. Finally he brought their wineglasses and sat down, taking her onto his lap.

She sighed and hid her eyes from him for a long moment as the warmth and reassurance of his arms flooded through her.

'It's hard to come down sometimes without feeling as if you're falling down a cliff,' he said barely audibly as he stroked her hair. 'Especially when it's so perfect.'

She closed her eyes in exquisite relief. 'That's exactly how I felt. As if I was falling through space, alone.'

He tilted her chin and kissed her lips until her lashes fluttered up and she drank in those smoky-grey eyes, the star-shaped scar which she touched again with her fingertips, then trailed her fingers down the lean lines of his face. 'I was also wondering what to do with myself while you're away.'

He captured her fingers and kissed them. 'I'll only be gone for three days.'

'That could feel like a millennium.'

'It could, I agree,' he conceded gravely. 'Why don't you come with me?'

She sat up and reached for her glass, giving him his at the same time. 'I don't have a reservation, for one thing—'

'I'm sure I could arrange that.'

She looked at him slightly askance. 'I don't know why but I believe you. Uh, no, I can't leave work at the moment—'

'Only one of those three days is going to be a working day.'

'Not for me, sadly, I need to work right through this weekend but—' she sipped her wine, then rested back against him '—the real reason is that I don't have the energy, moral fibre, presence of mind or whatever—to go anywhere at the moment, let alone Singapore.'

He laughed softly. 'Believe me, it's going to take considerable internal fortitude for me to go anywhere.'

She sipped some more wine then said abruptly, 'Did you know this was going to happen tonight?'

'No. Did you?'

'No,' she said slowly. 'Although I've spent all week wondering about it, and, if it did, what it means?'

'That we could be falling in love?'

A tremor ran through her and she turned her head to stare into his eyes. 'Yes. Oh, *yes*, but...' She stopped.

'It mightn't be a good idea to rush into anything?' She saw those grey eyes narrow as he spoke, and an expression she couldn't decipher shadow them for a moment before a flicker of amusement glinted. Then he added, 'I think that's very sensible, Miss Harris. Very wise and thoroughly Domenica.'

She said nothing, then a faint smile curved her lips. 'Which just goes to show you don't know Domenica as well as you think, Angus.'

'In what respect?' he queried.

'Well, there's a certain area of this Domenica that tells her she should, if she had any sense at all...' she paused and arranged her expression to severity '...put a halter on you and drag you to the nearest altar, Mr Keir.'

There was dead silence, then he started to laugh softly. 'There's a certain area of this man,' he responded finally, 'who will always love you for saying that.' He pulled her close and kissed her.

After that, all the constraint she'd felt disappeared and she was able to eat her supper as they sat side by side, talking desultorily. But it was warm, and wonderful in its own way, and this night, she was later to realize, typified their relationship. The natural, humorous togetherness that was so warming but such a contrast to the sheer fireworks of their physical passion for each other.

'I have to go,' he said at last, looking at his watch. 'And you should go back to bed.' He stood up and helped her to her feet, then drew her into his arms again.

'Mmm, I will,' she murmured as she clasped her hands behind his head, and rested her mouth on the corner of his. 'Go safely, Mr Keir.'

'You too, Miss Harris.' He stroked her hair, then drew his hands down her body intimately beneath the tissue-fine vanilla silk, so that she breathed erratically and buried her head in his shoulder, almost dizzy with the memories of what he'd done to her and how she'd reciprocated. Then, simultaneously, they drew apart—and smiled wryly at each other.

'Don't think this is easy,' he said.

'I'm trying not to think at all.' Her hands, hanging at her sides, were clenched into fists. 'But it might be an idea not to touch me.'

'I have to.' He reached for her hands and uncurled them, raising each palm to his lips for a fleeting moment, then he put them at her sides again, looked into her eyes and said barely audibly, 'I'll be back, Domenica. Nothing could keep me away.' And this time he did go.

She went back to bed and fell asleep almost at once. Nor did she wake until about ten o'clock and only then because someone was ringing her doorbell.

It turned out to be a florist delivery person, she discovered as she opened it, clutching her robe around her and trying to gather back her hair—bearing a huge bunch of roses although no card. But the most amazing thing about them, apart from their perfume and the cool,

velvety perfection of their petals, was their colours—pink, white and raspberry—as if they
had been chosen to match a room, her bedroom.

A coincidence? she wondered as she drifted
back to that room with the flowers in her arms.
Or a deliberate choice to celebrate what had
happened here?

'I think so,' she said aloud and buried her
face amongst the petals. 'I also think I can't
remember being so happy, before. You might
have made a new woman of me, Angus Keir.'
She lifted her face and smiled ruefully. 'To
think how antagonistic I was! Oh, well, thank
heavens I saw the light.'

And she took her roses away to find them a
vase, then she showered again and went to
work with an extra spring in her step, and not
the slightest intimation that one single rosebud
would one day bring her the kind of pain she
could never remember before.

Over the next weeks they spent all their free
time together.

And she discovered lots of little things about Angus Keir. That he might have thought he was doing something else with his life apart from making money, but he still spent an enormous amount of time either travelling or working, being one of them.

But it was the insights she gained into his background that she found fascinating. Such as, despite having a scanty schooling, he had a degree in economics. Such as, despite his millions, being unable to see any food go to waste and being an absolute whiz at fixing just about anything…

'You must have managed to teach yourself a lot,' she said to him once. It was a Sunday morning, they'd slept in at her apartment after a late night dining and dancing, and were having a late, lazy breakfast while they read the papers. It was the speed with which he read that prompted her comment.

He looked up. He wore shorts and no shirt, was barefoot. 'I did. I was lucky, my father was a great reader—it was about his only indulgence. He ordered books by the sackful, fiction and non-fiction on all sorts of subjects and

I read every one of them. He was quite cultured and he had a very enquiring mind.'

'Which he passed on to you, I gather.'

'Yep.'

'What about music?' she asked. 'Where did that love come from?'

'I didn't see it in my father so I guess it came from my mother. But the owner of the property used to love music and he also, well—' Angus paused '—he and my father fell out frequently on the subject of how I should be brought up. He even offered to send me away to school. And he found a second-hand but full set of encyclopedias for one of my birthdays.'

Domenica stared at him with an image in her mind's eye of a little boy thirsting for knowledge and reading everything he could lay his hands on.

'So, not only self-made,' he interrupted her reverie with a wry little grin, 'but self-taught.'

'Very seriously bright, however,' she commented.

'I don't know about that but very seriously...something at this moment,' he murmured, casting the paper aside and feasting his gaze on her. All she wore was a wine-coloured short silk nightgown with shoestring straps. And he held out his hand to her.

She joined him on the settee, to find that shortly thereafter she was wearing nothing at all, and he said with soft satire, 'That's the word I was looking for—very seriously deprived, Miss Domenica Harris.'

'It's only been six hours at the most,' she pointed out.

'Are you telling me it's too soon for you?' he queried and ran his hands down her legs.

'It could be. I'm a once-a-night kind of girl, I suspect, or once in a certain set of hours, if you know what I mean, but if things are that serious for you, I'd be happy to, well—' She paused.

'Accommodate me?' he suggested.

She saw the sheer devilry dancing in his eyes, and grimaced. 'Why do I get the feeling I'm going to be made to eat those words?'

'I have no idea,' he replied and moved his hands to her upper body.

'Oh, yes, you do, Angus Keir,' she accused. 'If for no other reason than that, as well as being seriously bright, I get the feeling you can never resist a challenge.'

'Ah…' he looked thoughtful '—you could be right.' And proceeded to demonstrate that she was.

So that, on finding herself far from being accommodating but quite the opposite, which was quivering with desire in his arms, she asked him breathlessly just how he'd done it.

'It's all in the preparation, ma'am,' he replied seriously.

'Did…did you read up about this kind of expertise, Angus?'

His eyes danced for a moment. 'That's classified, ma'am.'

One evening he came to her apartment for dinner—she'd invited Natalie and her boyfriend as well—to find her almost tearing her hair out.

'What?' he said as soon as she opened the door to him.

'My waste-disposal unit is blocked,' she answered tragically. 'My sink is almost overflowing; it's *impossible* to prepare a meal without a usable sink; no one seems to know if I need a plumber or an electrician and I can't get anyone until tomorrow anyway!'

'Domenica, calm down,' he said laughingly. 'You look quite wild.'

She looked down at herself. She hadn't changed out of the cream jeans and taupe blouse she'd worn to work, but somehow, in her exertions, her blouse had come adrift at the waist and unbuttoned lower than was seemly, her feet were bare and her hair was riotous. 'I feel wild,' she said bitterly. 'I feel helpless and useless and that *really* annoys me.'

He put his arms around her, and said, with his lips twisting wryly, 'And here I was thinking that nothing could shake you out of your almost regal composure, Domenica—well, almost nothing.' He glinted a meaningful little look down at her.

She moved restlessly and a little surge of colour entered her cheeks. 'That's the last thing I need to be reminded of at the moment, Angus,' she told him a little bitterly, however.

'Very well,' he murmured. 'But may I expect a reward for fixing your waste-disposal unit?'

'A...what kind of reward? And you don't know that you *can* fix it!'

'I'd be prepared to bet on it, though,' he drawled.

She hesitated, staring up at him half frowning, half calculatingly. 'So, I ought not to sign my life away in the matter of a reward, in other words?'

He laughed softly. 'That's rather perceptive of you.'

'OK—' she pretended to consider '—how about—? Ah! I think I'd like to surprise you. It is getting late,' she added.

'And with that I'll have to be content, no doubt,' he said ruefully.

'Um...maybe this will...lighten your labours.' She stood on tiptoe and kissed him lingeringly.

'I'll look upon it as a down payment,' he offered. Then he hugged her and recommended she go and have a shower and get changed.

Ten minutes later he brought her a glass of champagne and the news that the disposal unit was fixed. After Natalie and her boyfriend had left, much later in the evening, she offered him his reward, in the form of demonstrating just how a pashmina could be worn with nothing else, which, predictably, led to a mutually rewarding encounter.

As she lay in his arms afterwards, drowsily, she did say that it could have been a piece of luck that had seen him fix the disposer so easily.

'Don't you believe it,' he responded, and over the following weeks proved it when he fixed her clothes dryer, which had mysteriously ceased to operate, for her, and then her answering machine and her video recorder. Not that the video recorder had required fixing, just the understanding of how to operate it, as he had pointed out.

'Glory be, do I ever need a man like you in my life!' she'd enthused.

'I have to agree...' he'd looked devastatingly amused '...because I don't think I've ever seen anyone who can get into quite such a state over or have as little understanding of mechanics or electronics as you do.'

'Just concentrate on the things I do well, then,' she'd recommended.

They'd been having this conversation on the way to a party but they never did get to it, because he'd turned the Range Rover round and driven them straight back to his penthouse.

CHAPTER FIVE

THREE months after Domenica and Angus had first slept together, Natalie said, 'Domenica, it is your birthday today, isn't it?'

'Yep! Twenty-six today,' Domenica sang, then paused to lift her head from the keyboard she was working on and eye her friend and partner suspiciously. 'Am I going mad or did you not give me this card—' she picked up a birthday card '—and this gorgeous pair of embroidered evening gloves just this morning and *for* my birthday, Nat?'

'I did. However they might pale…but before I go into that—' Natalie didn't turn from the window she was looking out of '—have you heard from Angus today?'

'No, but I will,' Domenica said happily. 'He's due back from Malaysia this morning.'

'He sure gets about,' Natalie commented. 'But, Dom, is it or is it not a fact that your car

161

has broken down again and quite seriously this time?'

Domenica nodded, her happiness changing to rueful gloom. 'I really think it's had it and I should get a new one but how to afford it is another matter...oh, well, I'll wait until I get a quote for the repairs.'

'I don't think you'll need to bother,' Natalie remarked.

Something alerted Domenica at last. 'What do you mean?' she asked slowly

'Unless someone else in the building is having a birthday today, your car problems could be at an end.'

Domenica got up and walked over to the window. 'I still don't know what you're talking but...' She stopped on an indrawn breath, for down in the street directly below the studio stood a brand-new silver hatchback car, gift-wrapped in pink ribbon with a huge multi-loop bow on the roof, plus silver heart-shaped balloons printed with the words 'Happy Birthday'.

And although the full glory of the bow and balloons was better seen from directly above, there was a little crowd gathered around the car.

'I don't believe it,' she whispered. 'He wouldn't—it must be someone else's.'

'I doubt it—I do believe it,' Natalie said, breaking into spontaneous laughter at last, and she hugged Domenica impulsively. 'Kiddo,' she added, 'have you got this guy *in*! Not that it surprises me. And if you were stunning before, you're sensational now so I'd say it's fairly mutual.'

Domenica put her hands to her hot cheeks and her eyes were horrified. 'But he can't do this. You don't give people cars for their birthdays, not unless they're...you just don't!' she protested.

'Pet, listen to me,' Natalie advised wisely, 'there's a whole world of girls out there who would kill to have a man make that kind of a statement just once in their lives, me included. And I've seen you walking on air for the last months, I've seen you get off the phone after talking to him with your head in the clouds, I've seen the two of you together—don't knock it. He's dynamite, so are you, and it's his way of expressing it. Besides, what could be more practical? And it's not as if he can't afford it! I'll give you a hand to unwrap it before it creates a traffic jam.'

'No, look, I better check first,' Domenica protested, and reached for the phone, only to put it down in frustration because he wouldn't be in his office yet. But at that moment a package was delivered by hand. Inside was a set of car keys on a gold keyring with the letters D and H beautifully engraved on it.

'I rest my case,' Natalie said as she stared at it in Domenica's hands.

'I wish you hadn't said that!'

Natalie raised an eyebrow at her.

'Angus said the same thing to me once,' she explained, but as Natalie looked mystified she shrugged. 'It doesn't matter. How many people are there down there now?'

'About fifty, all laughing and joking. And there are several cars stopped.'

'Nat, would you…? I—'

'There's a traffic warden stopping now, two actually.'

Domenica swore beneath her breath. 'All *right*! I'll come.'

Her mother was giving a formal party in honour of Domenica's birthday that night. The Rose Bay home had not been sold yet but there were several people interested in it and Barbara had pleaded with her daughter to be allowed to give what might be the last grand party in what had been her home for so long.

Domenica had succumbed, not because she wanted a grand party but because her mother was still a changed, much happier person who nevertheless adored grand parties and deserved at least one last one in her grand home. But she'd insisted that Barbara hire a firm of caterers for the thirty people invited for cocktails and a buffet supper.

And when she got home to her apartment after work, having driven herself there in the new car although in a state of suspended unreality, there was a message on her answering machine from Angus via his secretary. To say that, with much regret, he'd been unavoidably delayed and could he meet her at Rose Bay instead of collecting her from the apartment as had been previously arranged?

Domenica sat down on her bed and felt a prickle of annoyance. She was quite used to receiving messages from his secretary on her answering machine, for he was quite frequently 'unavoidably delayed' but she'd taken it in her stride until now. The same thing sometimes happened to her.

Now, though, it not only pricked her, it actually incensed her, she discovered, that he couldn't pick up the phone himself to leave a message. But not only that. She had really wanted to be able to give him back his car and make him understand why she was doing it before they went to her birthday party.

Then it crossed her mind to wonder whether this unavoidable delay had been manufactured so she couldn't do just that. She ground her teeth but time was running away from her and she reluctantly started to dress, but thought as she did so—I'll take a taxi!

Half an hour later, showered, perfumed, moisturized and beautifully groomed, she stared at her reflection in the cheval-mirror and was pleased.

Her outfit was two-piece, a strapless bustier in a coppery apricot, and it came down to a point at the waist. The long skirt in the same Thai silk fitted superbly to her knees, then flared slightly towards the floor. It was an elegant creation and she wore an antique rose gold chain with a ruby pendant around her neck, and high-heeled bronze sandals.

But instead of leaving her hair loose as she'd taken to doing for the last two months, she brushed its rich darkness back severely and rolled it into a pleat. Which made her look regal, composed and slightly older, exactly what she'd been aiming for. So, Angus Keir, she said to her reflection, no mermaids or wild gypsy girls tonight. Be warned, mate!

But a shower of rain on her bedroom window alerted her to the fact that it had started to pour and she suddenly remembered her decision to take a taxi, but knew from long experience that nothing put a premium on taxis more than heavy rain, especially at this time of the day, especially on a Friday evening. She tried all the same but the taxi company warned it would be at least half an hour.

Make that an hour, she mused, and sighed, because there was no help for it but to drive the birthday present car—she was already running late. She picked up the heavy keyring, her purse and her pashmina, hesitated for a last moment and let herself out.

It was a difficult drive in the heavy rain and more so because of her preoccupation that ran along the lines of—how could three months of bliss with Angus Keir suddenly produce this situation that was a little like running into a brick wall? It had been bliss, Natalie was right. Nor had she made any attempt to hide it from her family or her world. She and Angus were an item, there was no doubt.

They'd been seen out and about at the races, at concerts, at restaurants, at other social events. They'd been photographed together several times, at an art gallery exhibition, crewing on a yacht on the harbour and at a fund-raising walkathon for disabled children. They'd even laughed together at one caption that had read, 'Is this boy-from-the-bush

Angus Keir's uptown girl?' What they hadn't been able to do at times was hide the electricity that ran between them.

Nor had the passion they experienced when they were together and alone diminished. It had grown, if anything.

And both Barbara and Christy Harris were delighted for her, she had no doubt, although her mother was starting to make remarks along the lines of when would the wedding bells be chiming?

Causing her, Domenica reflected as she swung into her mother's street, to laugh and dismiss these comments with a shrug, and not even think twice about them, but now...

She clicked her teeth in genuine frustration because the dark green Range Rover was already parked in the drive. There was no room for her car in the drive. It was still raining, although not as heavily but she hadn't brought an umbrella. So she did the only thing possible: she wrapped herself in the pashmina, covering her hair as well, and made a dash for the front door.

It was just about to close as she got there—on her mother and Angus—but it swung open again revealing her, flushed and breathless with raindrops shimmering on the pashmina.

Her mother was delighted and kissed her warmly, wishing her happy birthday. But Angus didn't turn to follow her mother in for a long moment. His gaze drifted over Domenica instead and in a way that stilled her hands as she went to unwrap herself.

Then he said quietly, 'You look like a mysterious but exquisite Indian princess, Domenica. Happy birthday, my dear.'

'Thank you.' She unwound the wrap with unsteady hands. 'And thank you very much for the thought, Angus, but I can't accept the car.' She handed him the heavy gold keyring.

He had no choice but to take it as Christy descended on them and flung her arms around Domenica. And as the strains of 'Happy Birthday' struck up as Christy led Domenica into the lounge and thirty or so people raised their champagne glasses and sang to her, he merely slipped the keys into his jacket pocket.

Nor was there much he could do while she moved around the room and greeted everyone, mostly old friends of the family who not only embraced her, but showered her with gifts. In fact he stayed with Christy, who always found plenty to talk to him about and had even persuaded him to give her some insights into his life for her boss's book.

But when things settled down, he and Domenica played a cat-and-mouse game for the rest of the evening.

When they happened to be together at the buffet table, he said barely audibly, 'I gather I've offended you, Domenica?'

She shrugged as she piled savoury rice and butterfly prawns in a crisp golden batter onto her plate. 'I'd have been happier with a bunch of flowers, Angus.'

'But less mobile,' he suggested dryly.

She glinted him a proud blue look from beneath her lashes. 'That's my business.' And she drifted away.

They came together again over dessert. It was impossible to ignore him without causing comment and without worrying her mother, who was absolutely radiant in sapphire-blue silk but still capable of discerning signs of discord in her elder daughter. Especially on this night that she'd planned, as she told everybody in a toast to Domenica, not only as a birthday celebration, but as a mark of gratitude for all *both* her daughters, Domenica and Christabel, had done for her after Walter Harris's death.

So Domenica made room for Angus at a small round table and greeted him with a smile as he sat down. She even conducted a lively conversation with him and the two other people sharing the table, until they both left to acquire some more of the fabulous desserts on offer.

'I could have given you diamonds or pearls,' he murmured, as if nothing had happened to interrupt their earlier words. 'What would have been the difference?' He raised his gaze to hers and studied her with a faint smile, but a decided glint of irony in his eyes.

'Nothing.' She ate some lemon meringue and dabbed a napkin to her lips. 'I would have returned them as well.'

'So what am I allowed to give you?'

'Flowers—I told you about those—books, music...' she waved a hand '...maybe another elephant since I happen to collect them. I wouldn't have minded a small painting of an elephant, say, or—'

'Is this a lesson in good taste for the boy from the bush from his uptown girl, by any chance, Domenica?' he broke in, still smiling at her but like a tiger roused from somnolence by a form of prey in its sights.

'No, Angus.' She said it steadily despite regretting certain things, and forced herself to go on. 'It's a lesson in how not to make a woman feel "kept". That's all.'

'So it's OK to buy a mistress or a wife a car?' he suggested. 'But not OK to devise a way to help a lover out of an awkward situation in the most practical way possible? Although I did get it gift-wrapped.'

She closed her eyes briefly. 'It was lovely, the way it was wrapped, it was...' She stopped helplessly. 'And it was thoughtful too,' she went on presently, 'but...it also represents close to thirty thousand dollars. Don't you see?'

'I see your mother approaching,' he said, and stood up. 'Can I get you some more dessert, Domenica? Mrs Harris, please take my chair. I'm off to appease my sweet tooth again. Can I get you anything? And may I compliment you on a wonderful celebration of Domenica's birthday?'

Barbara declined but sank down beside her daughter looking supremely gratified. 'He's so nice,' she said enthusiastically. 'And you two are so right for each other! I must admit I was wondering whether he'd give you an engagement ring for your birthday.' She looked at Domenica questioningly.

It struck Domenica like a blow as she sought for the words to answer her mother, that beneath all her objections was this one root cause of her unhappiness. That she too, in some secret recess of her heart, had been hoping for an engagement ring to celebrate her birthday and their love.

She swallowed something non-existent in her throat and said with an effort at gaiety, 'Mum, it's only been three months!'

'Well, I know that...' Barbara spread her hands and looked about to deliver herself of a lecture on the subject, then apparently changed her mind as she said, 'But he must have given you something! Don't keep me in suspense, darling.'

'I...he...gave me a new car,' Domenica said helplessly. 'Delivered to work all wrapped up in pink ribbons and silver balloons. I...' But she couldn't go on.

Barbara blinked several times. Then she said in awestruck tones, 'He didn't!'

'Believe me, he did,' her daughter replied, 'but I'm—'

'But that's wonderful! It's exactly what you need and how romantic to wrap it up in pink ribbons and silver balloons. You're a very lucky girl, Domenica.'

Unbeknownst to Barbara, Angus had come back and was standing behind her as she said this, so he not only heard it, he saw Domenica's look of pure frustration at, he guessed, not receiving support from the one direction she might have felt she could rely on it.

Nor had she seen him either when she said to Barbara, 'But…but it's such a lot of money, I mean—'

'That's all relative, darling,' Barbara objected. 'He's got an awful lot of money! What did you expect? A bunch of flowers? I hardly think he'd do that when he's obviously infatuated.'

'You and Nat are of the same mind,' Domenica said darkly, then looked up at last to see him.

He said nothing, did nothing, but he might as well have shouted *I rest my case*, she thought dismally as their gazes clashed.

But she played out her part until midnight, her part of a dutiful, delighted daughter, that was, although she thanked her lucky stars that dancing was not on the agenda. She also got a surprise. Christy introduced her to a young man with curly brown hair and a shy smile who had arrived late, a young man who had difficulty tearing his eyes from her little sister who was quietly glowing in an off-the-shoulder aqua gown that was richer and more revealing that her normal style.

But before Domenica had a chance to find out more, at a quarter to midnight coffee and champagne were served and a birthday cake with twenty-six candles was carried aloft into the darkened room. Once again everyone sang to her, but as she blew out the candles and cut the cake Angus was by her side, and he was the one to make a speech this time.

'I'd like to propose a toast to Domenica, who brightens most people's lives, I suspect,' he said to the room at large, and then, pinning her beneath his smoky-grey gaze, added quietly although quite audibly, 'but especially mine.'

'Hear, hear!' everyone chorused enthusiastically, but not only that—with the special sort of twinkle and fondness people bestowed on a couple in love.

'You're taking something for granted, aren't you?' Domenica said tautly, about half an hour later, seated beside him in the Range Rover.

'You wanted to stay on?' he queried with an undercurrent of irony. 'Everyone else was leaving.'

She refused to look at him. Not only had everyone else been leaving but he had extricated her smoothly and arranged with Christy to drive the new car in off the street, when there was room to get it into the garage. 'I didn't mean that,' she said.

'You better tell me what you did mean,' he said briefly.

'Don't be so sure that I aim to brighten up your life at the moment, Angus,' she recommended crisply. 'Where are we going?'

'My place,' he replied. 'The walls are thicker should you feel inclined to indulge in a—in our first domestic, Domenica.'

She set her teeth, tempted to scream and shout at him for not even trying to understand her feelings, when he pulled something out of his pocket and dropped it into her lap.

'I wanted to give you this in private,' he said coolly.

It was a small gift box and when she untied the gold string and lifted the lid it was to see a tiny, exquisitely wrought gold filigree brooch, an elephant—with sapphire-blue eyes. She stared down at it in the palm of her hand, then turned her head to stare out of the window so that he couldn't see the tears running down her cheeks. And they drove the short distance to his penthouse in silence as she grappled with the turmoil of her emotions.

She knew his penthouse well now—it was almost like a second home.

It was spacious and luxurious as well as professionally decorated. And the room they used most, apart from the main bedroom, was the den with its dark green walls and matching leather couches, its coppery-pink wall-to-wall carpet and collection of art. It was where they played chess, or listened to music. It was where they often ate meals on trays, watching television or reading. It was where, sometimes, they made love.

It was where he ushered her after their mostly silent drive back from her birthday party. Where he pulled off his jacket and slung it across the back of a chair, and asked her if she'd like anything.

'No, thank you.' Her voice was uneven and strained as she watched him undo his tie and consign it to the chair where his jacket lay.

'I gather I've now offended you,' she added, 'and I feel awful, especially in light of this.' She held up the gift box with the elephant in it. 'But I don't want a car from you, Angus, because—it just doesn't feel right.'

'No one else seems to share your opinion.'

'It's no one else's business but mine,' she said, then closed her eyes frustratedly. 'How can I make you understand? I don't want to have to be grateful to you for anything other than you yourself, and what we mean to each other.' Her lashes lifted and she stared at him.

There were about two feet of coppery-pink carpet between them but it might as well have been a mile. She could see it in the hard set of his mouth, and hear it when he drawled, 'You don't think it might mean something to me to know you're worried about having to afford a new car?'

'I'm not *that* worried—yes, it's a capital expenditure I didn't particularly want to have to make at the moment,' she conceded, 'what with extra wages to pay, new machines and before the profits start to roll in on the new line, if they do, but I'd have worked something out. I'm not destitute.'

'Is that how I've made you feel?'

She sighed and sat down. 'I just feel...' She stopped.

'Beholden,' he supplied and sat down beside her. 'What if I were to offer you the car on a lease basis? You could write off part of the payments as a legitimate expense since you also use it as a delivery vehicle.'

Her eyes widened. 'Would you?'

'I've got the feeling I might have to,' he said dryly.

'I...would...feel happier about that,' she said awkwardly. 'It was a possibility that had crossed my mind, anyway—I mean, to lease a vehicle in the interim.'

He watched her steadily.

'But I'm sorry if I've hurt your feelings,' she went on.

He said nothing for an age, then a corner of his mouth twitched. 'There's a way they could be restored.'

'Please tell me what it is?' She looked at him innocently.

His eyes narrowed, then he got up, dimmed the lights and put a CD on. When he came back, he held a hand down to her and said gravely, 'May I have this dance, ma'am?'

She rose and went into his arms.

'I was wondering whether your mother would arrange some dancing tonight,' he said into her hair as they swayed to the music.

'I was thanking heaven she hadn't,' Domenica replied.

He lifted his head and looked down at her amusedly. 'Why?'

'Because it's impossible to maintain a proper sense of grievance towards you, Mr Keir, when I'm dancing with you.'

'I see.' He ran his fingers through her hair and pulled out the pins. 'Are you telling me that if I'd waited until this moment you would have accepted the car?'

'No. But it would have been a whole lot harder not to.'

'What about this—moment?' He slid his hands around her back and felt for the zip of her bustier. 'It occurred to me during the course of the evening that this garment was in fact two garments. And that you might not be wearing anything beneath the top part.' He pulled down the zip and the bustier came away from her body in his hands. 'I was right.' He let it flutter to the floor.

'I'm not sure that it was right and proper to be having those kind of thoughts during the evening and in my mother's living room,' she said a little raggedly as his palms came up to cover her breasts.

'I have those kind of thoughts about you, Domenica, morning, noon and night. I have them whether you're there or not. Would you have been able to say no in these circumstances?' He withdrew his hands to her waist, and they danced, but his heavy-lidded gaze was on the way her breasts moved and the way the velvety tips had opened beneath his hands.

Domenica stilled slowly. To be half naked in his arms like this was interfering with her breathing and causing a riot of sensation to course through her. But it was also a challenge, she knew.

'Yes, I would have,' she murmured huskily with her head back so she could look straight into his eyes, 'although it would have been even harder. But now I'm free to tell you that I love dancing with you like this. It crossed my mind the first time I ever did dance with you, in fact, that it might be very special if we were somewhere quite private.' And she smoothed her hands up his arms, cupped his face, then leant forward to kiss him lightly before she closed her eyes and started to sway to the music again.

'How did this happen?'

It was Angus who posed the question with his head propped on a hand as he lay beside her in a vast rumpled bed beneath a pale grey-and-white-striped percale sheet.

Sunlight was streaming into the room, warming the grey-limned woodwork and glinting on the silver lamp stands and ornaments. The bed itself was on a dais surrounded by a sea of velvety pewter carpet, the windows were framed with grey-and-white patterned silk curtains, and Mrs Bush maintained several pots of magnificent, real madonna lilies around the room.

Domenica had drawn a stunned breath when she'd first seen this bedroom but Angus had laughingly denied any responsibility for it. It had been like this when he'd bought the penthouse, he'd said. It was like a royal apartment in a palace, she'd responded, and added that she'd never slept in a bed on a dais that looked fit for a princess. To which he'd replied that he was just as comfortable sleeping on the ground so it was all a bit lost on him, but he was only too happy if it made her feel like a princess.

That was the first time it had crossed Domenica's mind to wonder about the other women there must have been in his life, and to acknowledge that she didn't know a great deal about Angus Keir...

But on this morning, as he posed a question to her, those kind of thoughts were far from her mind.

'How did it happen? If you mean that we've woken at the crack of dawn after a very late night—could it be that, under the weight of certain other things we had on our minds, we neglected to close the curtains?' she suggested gravely.

He eyed her. His dark hair was hanging in his eyes and there were blue shadows on his jaw. Then he drew the sheet away and traced his fingers down between her breasts. 'How did we achieve that state of mind—quite contrary, incidentally, to the way we arrived here last night—is what I meant, Miss Harris?'

'Ah!' Domenica wrinkled her nose. 'You very wisely gave into the force of my arguments, Mr Keir—could that have been how it happened?'

'I don't know about wise...' his fingers strayed to her nipples '...but I have to accept that I gave into the force of something.'

'If you...keep doing that,' she said with a catch in her voice, 'I will be the one giving in. May I make a suggestion?'

'On one condition—that it doesn't involve leaving this bed in the immediate future,' he said, and allowed those wandering fingers to roam lower down her body.

'Far from it.' She moved restlessly and gasped.

'You were about to say?' he murmured, transferring that smoky-grey gaze to hers so that she could see the teasing glint in his eyes.

'Angus—I have no idea,' she conceded, 'but don't imagine I intend to take this lying down.' And she swept the sheet aside, sat up, and eased herself onto him. 'There,' she said, not without a glint of her own, a spark of triumph in the depths of her blue eyes before she veiled them with her lashes, and propped her chin on her fists, on his chest.

She felt his silent laughter jolt his chest. Then he said, 'All right, you've got me where you want me, Miss Harris. What do you intend to do with me?' But his hands were already cradling her hips.

'Keep you in suspense,' she replied mysteriously.

'Is this to be another test of wills?' he suggested.

'Well,' she temporized, 'perhaps. I like being here. It gives me a sense of power. Of course, I have to admit I'm a slave to the near

perfection of your body, Mr Keir, but this position gives me the freedom to—express it.'
She moved on him, voluptuously and wan-
tonly, and had the satisfaction of hearing him
groan softly. 'See what I mean?' she added,
her eyes alight with laughter now.

'Yes, only too well.' His expression was
rueful. 'However, I have to point out that I can
only take so much of this, Miss Harris.'

'That's a pity!' She said it gaily and started
to kiss him, then stopped abruptly. 'Then
again,' she whispered and stared searchingly
into his eyes, 'so can I—only take so much.
Angus—' she shuddered as he suddenly held
her hard to him '—why do we do this to each
other?'

He didn't answer her question until they
came down from that exposed peak they still
reached together after three months. Until she
was curled into his arms, still breathing un-
steadily and they were both soaked in sweat.
Then he said as he stroked her hair, 'We just
do, Domenica. About last night—'

But she put a finger to his lips. 'That's what I was going to say—let's leave last night and the car as a closed book.'

She saw something flicker in his eyes, perhaps indecision, and waited, suddenly taut and tense. But all he said, finally, was, 'Should we go for a swim? Then drive down to Lidcombe Peace for the night?'

She relaxed unwittingly. 'Sounds perfect. Yes, please.'

They had an invigorating surf, hot dogs and Coke for lunch, and arrived at Lidcombe Peace mid-afternoon.

This was another case of home from home for Domenica—in fact it could be said that she'd taken over the house, although all she'd done was take up from where her family had left off. She'd rehired the couple who'd looked after the house and garden for years. She was the one who decided what should be planted and when, that a new washing machine was essential; she was the one who had redecorated a spare bedroom for herself and Angus. And she kept an auxiliary wardrobe at Lidcombe Peace.

Because he was away so frequently, an old cottage far from the main house had been restored and a manager, a grizzled man in his sixties with a limp, installed to supervise the cattle and other aspects of the farm, such as the paddock of lucerne that had been planted and the two imperious alpacas that had also taken up residence—Domenica had named them Napoleon and Josephine, or Nap and Josie for short. But the manager's dearest love were the three horses Angus now had, and it was plain to see he was a horseman from way back.

But there was still the odd occasion when she felt like pinching herself at Lidcombe Peace, and felt a bit guilty that she should be able to enjoy it as if she'd never left it while her mother and Christy could not. Not that it seemed to bother them, and as she and Angus sat before the fire that evening it occurred to her that she hadn't seen as much of Christy as usual lately, and the young man who'd arrived late last night might be the reason why. She made a mental resolve to correct this state of affairs as soon as possible.

But thinking of Christy directed her thoughts to the party last night, and one fact that had become submerged in all the drama and emotion of the night. Yes, she had won the battle of the car, she reflected, but what about the stinging realization that what she'd really wanted was an engagement ring?

She glanced over towards Angus. He was stretched out full length on the settee wearing jeans and an old black T-shirt, reading the paper. She was sitting in a comfortable armchair with her feet drawn up on the seat and her chin resting on her knees. She'd already changed into her tartan flannelette pyjamas—summer was sliding towards autumn in a series of breathtakingly beautiful blue and gold days but with the nights on the Razorback Range turning distinctly chilly.

'Tell me about the other women you've had in your life, Angus?'

He lowered the paper and frowned at her over it. 'Why? And what brought that up?'

She shrugged, but glinted him a humorous little smile. 'Nothing in particular, I'd just like to know. According to my sister, until now I've always gone for more diffident men, for example.' She raised her eyebrows comically. 'I can imagine what you might say to that.'

He looked amused. 'Then I won't say it, but is that how *you* see it?'

She studied her toes. 'It's not how I saw it at the time. But my father was an academic and an historian so I met a lot of…not so much diffident men, but men wrapped up in their own academic world, perhaps. That's what I attribute it to now, although I guess Christy was right when she said that I've always been independent.' This time she grimaced. Then she looked at him directly. 'Did you ever have the kind of relationship we have, with another woman?'

'No. But, yes, there have been relationships.' He studied her thoughtfully. 'I can't say that there's been a pattern to them, though, of diffidence or otherwise.' He grinned fleetingly. 'Mind you, two redheads. My very first girlfriend when we were both about sixteen, and a fiery fling with a film star.'

Domenica stared at him wordlessly.

Until he said soberly, 'Are we not being honest, open and adult, Domenica? I thought that was the object of the exercise, and you were the one who brought it up.'

'I've just taken an instantaneous dislike to redheaded women,' she heard herself say, with some bemusement. 'But—' she frowned '—have there been lots of women?'

He paused, and smiled a little grimly this time. 'Would you like me to do a headcount? Have there been lots of men in your life even if they've all been wimps?'

'No,' she said steadily, refusing to let her anger mount, 'only one relationship, in fact, and it didn't last very long. By the way, who's refusing to be open, honest and adult now?' she added.

He sat up and dropped the paper to the floor. 'Domenica, there have been some—I'm thirty-six and I have a very normal admiration for the opposite sex—but, in fact, there haven't

been ''lots'', as you put it, because I've been
too busy. And there has been no one like you.'

He got up and came to sit on the footstool
she wasn't using and he put out his hand to
rest his fingers on her cheek. 'Some meant
more than others,' he went on quietly, 'but not
one of them did what you do to me, what we
do to each other, as you said only this morning.'

So why don't you ask me to marry you,
Angus? The question was in her mind and on
her lips but she couldn't bring herself to say
it.

Then she was glad she hadn't as he went on,
'You may not realize this but you weren't so
far off the mark with your ''Lone Ranger''
comment a couple of months ago. The only
things I had to rely on to get me out of the
back blocks of Tibooburra were my hands and
my brain, and a dream. But sometimes I look
back and wonder if it was worth it.'

'Why?' she whispered, with tears she
couldn't explain in her eyes.

'Why?' He turned his head and looked into
the fire. 'Self-reliance is a wonderful thing, un-

til it becomes impossible to surrender.' He looked back into her eyes and a wry smile lit his eyes. 'So I guess we're two of a kind, Domenica, and that's why it's so devastatingly explosive between us at times.'

She blinked and licked her lips as she digested what he'd said, the explicit and the implicit.

But before she had a chance to make real sense of it, he said, 'On the other hand, I'm tired, so are you and I can't think of anything nicer than to go to bed with you—just to hold you and be warm and together. Shall we?'

He didn't wait for an answer. He picked her up and carried her to bed, and did just that: held her and warmed her and stroked her hair until she fell asleep.

The next morning they carried on as normal.

If Domenica sometimes wondered about the boy from the bush in Angus Keir, and how his upbringing had shaped him, since the man reflected it so little, there was one area where you could easily imagine him in an outback scenario, and that was on a horse.

She rode well enough herself and had always loved horses but he was in a class of his own and so were his horses. Registered stock horses, all fillies, two were expertly trained and mouthed and a pleasure to ride. Which was what they did the next morning, Angus leading the third filly from his mount because she was still being broken in.

He'd explained to her the paramount abilities stock horses required—temperament, agility and safety—and how these traits were not only required of working horses that drafted cattle, but made them excellent polocrosse and campdrafting horses. There was a very good market for them, which was why he'd selected the three fillies with great care because he planned to breed from them.

She'd asked him once if he'd ever competed at campdrafting or polocrosse himself.

They'd been riding with Luke King, the manager, at the time and he and Angus had exchanged amused glances. Then Angus had said, 'Uh-huh. I bought my first truck with the cheque from a campdraft competition.'

'You wouldn't have been some kind of a champion at it?' she'd queried with her head to one side.

Luke had spat over his shoulder, and answered from beneath his beloved and battered Akubra hat, 'Only one of the best I ever saw.'

She'd later prised from Angus that he and Luke went all the way back to Tibooburra, and that he'd offered Luke the Lidcombe Peace job because of a broken leg that had set badly.

This early morning, however, they were alone. She had a quilted vest over her shirt, and jeans on, but Angus didn't seem to notice the chill and wore an old favourite, his khaki bush shirt, with his jeans. And he was talking encouragingly to the filly he was leading, as they rode into the main Hereford paddock.

Which gave her the opportunity to watch him without having to say much. Because, despite having presented a normal demeanour, there were all sorts of questions on her mind. Of course, she acknowledged, it was a pleasure just to be able to watch him.

He was hatless and superb. He rode his filly more with his body than his hands—you got the feeling he could ride with his hands tied behind his back—and you could see the strength in his lean, long lines. You could also hear the humour of what he was saying to the nervous filly he was leading—she was propping and rolling her eyes at the cattle—and how it was adapted to a feminine creature.

She found herself smiling at some of the things he said, such as, 'Sweetheart, it's all very well to look pretty and as if you'd like to pick up your skirts and run from these strange critters, but you need to show them you can out-think them any day of the week!' as he coaxed her along.

Then it occurred to Domenica that she herself might be a prime example of Angus Keir's way with women. And she forced herself to sift through what he'd said the night before. A warning? she wondered. A statement that, while things might be special between them, it was too soon to be making any plans for the future?

She moved her shoulders restlessly. It *was* only three months. But had his statement meant more than that? Surely marriage and children must feature on his agenda some time? She'd seen how well he got on with the Bailey children, who were regular visitors to Lidcombe Peace now. So why was that intrinsic wariness she'd had of Angus Keir back firmly in place now?

The only thing she resolved in the next few moments was that, however well-trained your horse was, if you were paying no attention to your riding at all you were likely to come a cropper. Which she did when a calf broke away from the herd, and her horse took off after it.

It wasn't a bad fall; the ground was thickly grassed and it acted as a cushion. She was only winded for a moment, then she got up to discover no broken bones, although she'd probably have some bruises. But Angus was at her side almost immediately and he dismounted, managed to handle both his horses with one hand and put the other arm around her.

And she could feel his heart thudding through his shirt almost as hard as hers was.

That did it, she thought later in the day, when she was home in her apartment, alone.

That moment of heart-stopping concern convinced her to stop tilting at windmills as he'd once accused her of. Yes, she could accept that he'd have to make adjustments, she of all people should be able to accept that. Yes, time was what they both needed, but perhaps he more than her. So what would a little time cost her?

Nothing, she decided. And ignored the inner voice that asked her what choice she had in the matter anyway.

CHAPTER SIX

FOUR months and most of winter went by.

They had a glorious holiday together skiing at Mount Buller, and one day a month or so later Angus simply rang Domenica at work and said he was picking her up in half an hour.

'What for?'

'I hate August,' he said down the line.

'Most people do in the southern hemisphere,' she responded with a laugh.

'Not necessarily closer to the equator.'

'Well, no, I guess they even appreciate it but…so?' She picked up a pencil and frowned at it.

'Let's just go.'

'To the equator? Angus, are you sickening for something?'

'Yes, for you, on a beach in a bikini on a tropical island with nothing to do but swim, eat and make love.'

Domenica hesitated. 'That sounds wonderful but—in half an hour? I...' she looked around her busy studio '...I...mean—'

'Did you not tell me your fashion empire is flourishing these days, Miss Harris?'

'Yes,' she said cautiously, 'but even if I could just walk out at the drop of a hat, I'd have to go home and pack—'

'It's all done.'

'What do you mean?'

'I've acquired everything you need for a tropical island, which is not such a lot— Domenica, you're not going to do the car act on me again, are you?' he enquired plaintively.

'Hang on—you mean you've bought me clothes?' she asked severely.

'Uh-huh. Much as I prefer you without them—well, that's not quite true,' he drawled down the phone. 'Taking you out of them is one of the great pleasures of life for me, as it so happens. Had you noticed?'

Domenica could feel the colour starting to rise in her cheeks and she looked around warily. To see that Natalie was studiously looking the other away.

'I'm also the man you once told you were a slave to the—er—perfection of—or something along those lines,' he went on conversationally. 'Not that I would have brought it up in the normal course of events, but I happen to remember exactly what you were doing when you said that. Do you? Perhaps I can refresh your memory—'

'All right,' her voice quivered as she broke in, 'I'll come but if that's not, well, blackmail I'll eat my hat.'

'Actually, it's something else,' he said and she could hear he was laughing. 'So? Half an hour?'

'Yes…' She put the phone down and hesitated before turning again to Natalie. 'I—'

'Just go,' Natalie said with an airy wave of her hand. 'Although why you have all the luck, I have no idea. All I ever get asked out to is the movies.'

Domenica flinched. 'But I feel—'

'Dom, I can cope, although it might be an idea to let me know where you are and how long you'll be away. Listen, let's just run through your diary before he arrives to sweep you off to the Tropics!'

Domenica paused in the act of starting to say that wasn't what she meant, and said instead, but with a curiously helpless little shrug, 'Thanks, pal.'

They spent five magic days and nights on Dunk Island, once home to that legendary beachcomber E. J. Banfield.

And all her misgivings, which she had difficulty putting a name to anyway, vanished for a time beneath the magic of Dunk with its exquisite Ulysses butterflies, marvellous rainforest that you could ride through on horseback, and lovely waters and beaches. They played golf on the six-hole course, she wore his choice of clothes and bikinis serenely—not hard to do because they were lovely anyway— and she pinned hibiscus blooms in the night darkness of her hair. But for the first time she saw an Angus Keir who needed help to relax.

'What is it?' she said on their third night when she woke up to find him, not in bed beside her, but on the veranda, looking out over Brammo Bay in the moonlight.

'Can't sleep, that's all,' he replied when she got up to join him and slipped an arm round his waist.

'Business on your mind?'

'No, not really.' He looked up towards the dark bulk of Mount Kootaloo. 'Beachcombing, I guess. Can you imagine what it would have been like for Banfield?'

'An enormous challenge, yes, also for Mrs Banfield—Bertha—to come here and start a new life, although she would have followed him to the ends of the earth from the inscription on her grave. Are you saying…' she paused '…you'd like to give it all up and do something similar?'

He rested his chin on the top of her head and she thought he sighed. 'Sometimes it's tempting.'

'A lot of people who come to Dunk might feel that way,' she said quietly. 'It's so beautiful, and it's romantic when you think of Banfield coming here because of his health, which he regained completely but…it could be a transient thing.'

'I'm sure you're right,' he said, but, she got the feeling, a little distantly. Then they went back to bed and she helped him to get to sleep in a time-honoured way.

The next morning, after breakfast, they were sitting at one of the tables beside the pool with its blue and black Ulysses butterflies painted on the bottom. The beach was right beside them, fringed with coconut palms growing in graceful curves towards the water, and the tide was in and rhythmically bathing the sand. No surf here within the protection of the reef, but the quality of light on the smooth, glittering surface of the water as it reflected the densely wooded slope of the island towards Mount Kootaloo was amazing.

Domenica had a turquoise bikini on beneath a filmy buttercup sarong tied between her breasts, large sunglasses and a peaked cap. Her hair was tied back and her pale skin was starting to acquire a golden bloom.

They planned to take advantage of the high tide and have a swim, then laze on the beach before playing six holes of golf. After lunch they planned to walk up to the farm and take the afternoon ride along the southern beaches.

But she said suddenly, 'Have you got an awful lot on your plate at the moment, Angus? Work-wise? Or should I say more than usual, which is a lot anyway?'

'Yep.' He pulled off his T-shirt. 'There's a merger coming up. Until now I've stuck to road transport and haulage but I'm thinking of buying a small freight airline and expanding it.' He moved his shoulders and grimaced.

'But you're not too enthused of the idea at the moment?' she suggested.

'I was very enthused of it and I will be again, no doubt,' he said ruefully and stood up and stretched, causing Domenica to marvel that she could still be affected by the sight of him wearing only bathers after over six months of being his lover.

'You know what happens when the tide goes out around here, don't you?' he went on.

'Yes, a mud-flat. Are you saying we should get in and swim before it's too late?'

'I am. I'm also suggesting we swim down to the jetty. Good for the figure.'

She looked down at herself and laughed. 'Am I getting fat?'

'Hardly.' He allowed his gaze to run over her as she released the sarong.

'That's a long swim!'

'I'll take you for a ride on a jet ski when we get there. We can go round Purtaboi.'

Purtaboi was the little island that danced in the bay. But, as Domenica looked out towards it and said she'd like that, it was in her mind suddenly to think that Angus might not only be affected by the magic of Dunk, but at a genuine crossroads in his life, another one. Buying Lidcombe Peace had been a crossroads for him but had it not come up to expectations or…?

'Let's go,' he said and jumped down onto the beach.

It was a thought she was only properly able to enlarge on while she dressed for dinner that night. Angus had gone to send some faxes from the office and she was to meet him in the lounge.

Even on Dunk it was cool in the evenings in August so she chose a long-sleeved denim blouse to wear with oyster, very fine cord trousers. Instead of tucking the blouse in, because it was bulky anyway, she wore it out with the silver chain belt that had come with the trousers slung loosely around her hips. And as she slid her feet into flat grey kid shoes she was struck again that he could have chosen, down to the shoes, things she not only loved but that fitted her perfectly.

But as she sat down at the dressing table to do her hair and face she couldn't avoid the unasked questions in her eyes as reflected in the mirror.

If this was a crossroad for Angus, and she could feel the tension in him even without his difficulty in sleeping and desire to be active all the time, was it anything to do with her? Had the time come, she wondered as she picked up her brush and stroked it through her hair, for a decision one way or another?

Then she realized she'd stopped brushing and was clenching the brush almost painfully in her fist. But what could she do, other than what she'd done these past four months, to help him make this decision and make it her way? Make some sort of a declaration of her own?

She put the brush down and stood up with a sigh. Because how she'd been, how they'd been together for the past months was, one would have thought, the only declaration that needed making.

He was waiting for her in the lounge and he stood up as he saw her approaching. There was no mistaking the salute in his eyes as they came together, nor the moment of intense focus they shared, as if the lounge, the pleasant music being played on the piano, the clink of glasses and the murmur of conversation might not have existed.

It's going to be all right, she told herself; it has to be.

But it wasn't.

Another two months went past, Angus appeared to get back to normal, which was to say he was also extremely busy, and their relationship pursued the same course it always had. The Rose Bay home was finally sold and Barbara and Christy moved to a town house. And Domenica's aerobics bodysuit became such a hit, she was flooded with orders and beseeched for more sportswear designs. She decided to call her label Aquarius.

Then two things happened. Christy confided to Domenica that she and Ian Holmes, the young man who had arrived late at Domenica's birthday party and who she now knew as a medical intern and thoroughly liked, were secretly engaged.

'Ian wanted to shout it from the roof-tops,' Christy said as she showed Domenica the sapphire engagement ring she wore on a ribbon around her neck, 'but I persuaded him to let me get Mum really settled first.'

Domenica hugged her little sister. 'I'm so happy for you, darling! He's such a honey.'

'Not that we plan to get married just yet. He's got another six months of his internship to go so we thought we'd wait until then. It's funny,' Christy added. 'I thought you and Angus might beat us to the draw.'

All Domenica had been able to say in response to the serious query in her sister's eyes was, 'It hasn't got to that stage yet, Christy.'

About a week later she and Angus spent the night in his penthouse, but when she woke the next morning he was gone and there was a note on the pillow to say that he'd forgotten to tell her he would be in Darwin and Perth for the next two weeks, but she'd looked so peaceful, he hadn't wanted to wake her.

Beside the note was a perfect pink rosebud.

Domenica sat up, pushed her hair back and looked around at the silver and grey perfection of his bedroom—suddenly sterile apart from the lovely bowl of pink roses on a table—and discovered herself to be weeping helplessly and racked by the kind of mental agony she'd never known.

But half an hour later she was showered and dressed, and she'd remade the bed with clean sheets as she always did for Mrs Bush. There was a note for Angus sealed into an envelope on the pillow, but the rosebud had been put back amongst the others in the vase. Then she went quietly around the apartment, gathering her belongings, a few books and sketch-pads, some CDs, some clothes. She put them in a green rubbish bag—thanking heaven that Mrs Bush hadn't arrived as yet—and, after a last look round, let herself out and dropped the keys she had to the penthouse into his mail box.

Two days later she was winging her way to Europe on a jet, with her mother.

They spent two months overseas ostensibly gathering fabrics and ideas but with Domenica, at least, trying to deal with a broken heart at the same time as she tried to make it a wonderful holiday for her mother.

Barbara had been deeply disturbed by Domenica's blunt announcement that she and Angus had broken up, but had been held mostly silent under the look of almost intolerable strain in her daughter's eyes.

It was in Italy that they made contact with a textile manufacturer whose father had been a friend of Walter Harris. Count Emilio Strozzi was fair and good-looking, about thirty, with a *palazzo* on the shores of a lake, unmarried and possessed of a roving eye. His factory also produced some of the most exciting fabrics Domenica had seen and they had a genuine rapport over this.

That Emil, as he'd told her to call him, should earnestly desire this rapport to extend to the personal soon became apparent to Domenica, but she laughingly withstood it for the three weeks they spent in Italy. That didn't stop Emil from wining and dining her or inviting her and her mother to the *palazzo* to meet his mother, and persuading them to spend a weekend with the family.

Nor could Domenica see any reason not to accept an invitation, extended by his mother, to attend an anniversary ball at the *palazzo*— the hundredth anniversary of the founding of the textile company.

What she failed to grasp, however, was that Emil was one of the country's most eligible bachelors, and that she would end up splashed over a variety of newspapers and magazines in her beautiful delphinium gown with Count Emilio Strozzi beside her and looking down at her in an unmistakable way. The gossip columns had a field day and produced more pictures of them dining together, with captions asking who was this stunning Australian girl who looked set to steal a favourite son?

But she managed to leave Italy without succumbing to Emil's machinations, and without breaking his heart either. Nor did she give the matter much further thought and it never entered her head that the gossip, or the pictures, would find their way home—but they did.

It was Natalie who alerted Domenica to the fact that she'd been romantically linked to an Italian count who looked almost as gorgeous as Angus Keir...although she'd bitten her tongue as soon as she'd said it.

But Domenica had only shrugged and smiled vaguely. 'Just wait until you see the gorgeous materials I bought from Count Emilio Strozzi, Nat. You'll drool!'

Natalie hesitated. 'Angus rang, you know, from Perth or Darwin or somewhere like that. The day after you left.'

Domenica said nothing.

'He said he kept getting your answering machine. Dom, why was it left to *me* to tell him where you were?'

Domenica looked up. 'I'm sorry, Nat. I...I did leave him a note but he wouldn't have got it until he got home.'

'I can't believe you let it end,' Natalie said sadly.

'*I* didn't...' Domenica stopped helplessly.

'So this Italian count was not the reason?'

Domenica blinked at her. 'Are you *joking*?' she asked incredulously.

Natalie gestured helplessly. 'It just, well, it could look that way.'

'It was nothing.' Domenica shrugged. 'His father knew my father and it was my mother who organized it, otherwise I'd have dealt with some employee, no doubt. And, apart from the odd dinner I had with him, my mother was there all the time, at the ball as well.'

'That's not quite the impression the pictures gave.'

Domenica clicked her tongue exasperatedly but left it at that.

She'd been home a few weeks when she was invited to a party given by a couple of friends who'd been overseas for two years and were celebrating their return. A married couple, they were both in television, Mark Dodson being a current affairs reporter and his wife, Sue, whom Domenica had been to school with, a director of documentaries. They were also a trendy couple, whose parties had been renowned before they'd left for the States.

Not that Domenica felt like partying, but she was genuinely fond of Sue and they were probably the only people in Sydney who wouldn't know of her connection with Angus. Nor did she imagine that both she and Angus could know the Dodsons without it having come out while they were together. But, perhaps most importantly, she had the feeling she had to do something to pull herself together and get herself going again.

Not that she felt like doing that either, but her state of mind was beginning to affect her creativity at a time when she really needed to take advantage of the hit she'd made in the sportswear arena.

It was to be a late afternoon barbecue and it was a beautiful Sunday afternoon. She donned an ivory linen blouse with short sleeves and a Peter Pan collar and a gathered, three-quarter-length skirt, black with ivory and taupe roses on it, and slid her feet into flat black shoes. Although it was January now, she decided to take her pashmina in case it turned cool, and she tied her hair back in a bronze scrunchie.

She'd made Sue some cheese straws, which she wrapped in red Cellophane and tied with a raffia bow, and a welcome home card, and she tied a similar bow around the neck of a bottle of champagne for Mark. And she drove out to Castle Hill in the silver hatchback Angus had given her for her birthday so many moons ago, it seemed, although it was now officially hers. After the sale of the Rose Bay house, in which she and Christy had had small shares, she'd used the money to buy the car from Angus.

The Dodsons had a few acres—they were both mad about horses—and a big garden. The barbecue was set up under some lovely old trees with lights strung through them. It was a warm reunion with lots of news to be told, including the most pertinent—that Sue was pregnant—and there were quite a few familiar faces amongst the twenty or so guests.

But it was while one guest was proposing a humorous toast to the Dodsons along the lines of—was this what maternity and paternity did to people? Turned them into barbecue hosts rather than hosts of the mad affairs they used to hold—that a latecomer arrived.

That was how Angus Keir saw Domenica Harris for the first time in more than two months—laughing and raising a champagne glass in a toast.

And he found himself thinking that she looked as she'd always looked: tall, willowy, a lovely carriage, that marvellous skin and beautifully defined jawbone, casual but elegant—in a word, sensational. And she was obviously enjoying herself. As if, he thought, the ending of their affair via a simple note thanking him for everything but telling him it was time for her to move on had taken not the slightest toll of her.

She turned as Sue hailed him and it gave him a sense of savage satisfaction to see her pale noticeably as her fingers also whitened around the stem of her glass.

Then Sue was making introductions all round and explaining that the Dodsons and Angus Keir had only met about a month ago at a polocrosse game.

Domenica found herself wondering dryly why she hadn't thought of that—then he was standing in front of her and she had to say something... 'Hi!' She turned to Sue. 'We have met—'

'Great!' Sue enthused. 'Then I'll leave Angus with you for a bit, Dom, while I start bringing out the food!'

'Oh—can't I help?'

'No, you just keep this gorgeous hunk happy, Dom,' Sue said with a twinkle, and quite unaware that she caused her friend to flinch inwardly as she waltzed away.

'*Met?*'

It was only one softly said word, but uttered with such insolent derision in his voice and eyes, Domenica trembled visibly and looked away. 'Angus, this isn't the time or the place to indulge in recriminations or whatever.'

'I agree,' he drawled. 'So I'll just run one thing past you before we become good, convivial little guests. I take it an Italian count is closer to your social standing than I was?'

She stared into his grey eyes, stunned into speechlessness. Then Mark joined them, the conversation turned to stock horses, and for the rest of what seemed like a never-ending evening they avoided any direct dealings with each other. To make things harder for Domenica, she had to watch Angus exerting his considerable charm over a colleague of Sue's, a lovely blonde woman about his own age who was unattached.

She left at the first opportunity to do it without seeming rude, and started to drive home feeling exhausted and as if she'd been through a wringer. But after a few miles she realized it was becoming difficult to steer the car and it dawned on her, to her horror, that she had a flat tyre. She managed to pull off the road and when she got out, there was the evidence of it to greet her eyes. She banged her fist on her forehead, then looked around.

She'd never changed a tyre in her life. It was very dark, although not that late, but the houses around were widely spaced because they were all on acreage and she couldn't see one light. It was also cold now and windy, and she wrapped her pashmina around her. Then a pair of headlights coming from the direction she'd come from lit the night and she found herself praying it was someone coming from the barbecue and not some dubious stranger.

In fact, it was a dark green Range Rover that drew up in front of her car, one she knew well, and no stranger who stepped out, causing her to wonder numbly whether this day had been somehow jinxed for her.

'Well, well,' Angus Keir said as he kicked the tyre she was standing beside, 'does this give you a sense of *déjà vu*, Domenica?'

'Yes, no, I mean—' She stopped helplessly.

He smiled tigerishly. 'I can imagine—twenty odd guests to choose from but it had to be me who came along to your damsel-in-distress situation. I have no doubt you're completely incapable of changing a tyre. But would you prefer it if I drove on, Miss Harris? There will be others coming but I'm not sure when.'

'No!' There was a little bubble of hysteria in her voice that she'd been unable to help and that he noted with a narrowing of his eyes.

'OK.' He shrugged. 'I don't suppose you've got a torch? Women rarely do have the essential items, but luckily enough I do.' He opened the hatch of the Range Rover and produced a powerful one which he gave her to hold. Then he opened her boot, assembled what he needed and started to change the tyre.

Of course he did it quickly and competently and, apart from remarking that she'd driven over a nail somewhere in her travels, in dead silence.

And as Domenica provided him with light she could think of something to say, but finding the courage to say anything seemed to be beyond her. Then it was done, her tools and the flat tyre were packed away and he was wiping his hands on his handkerchief.

'That should get you home, but I'd have the spare checked too. Goodnight—'

'Angus,' she broke in desperately, 'it's not what you thought!'

He lifted an eyebrow at her and directed a peculiarly meaningful look at her pashmina that brought back all sorts of memories to her and made her blush.

'A-about social standing or anything like that. It…it…' She stopped and swallowed. 'There was—'

'I don't really think this is the time or place for convoluted explanations, Domenica,' he broke in and looked around impatiently. 'If you're *sure* you want to explain anything, then come home with me so it can be done in some comfort, at least.'

'No…' But the sheer contempt in his eyes did two things: put some spirit back into her, although it also pricked her conscience. 'But if you'd like to come up to my apartment and have a cup of coffee with me, I would at least like to…explain.'

'Domenica, do you remember having dinner with me only, so you said, because you wanted to make amends for your mother's indiscreet tongue?' he taunted.

She set her mouth severely as they stared into each other's eyes. Then she flicked his torch off and handed it back to him. 'The offer is still open, Angus Keir,' she said flatly, 'but come, or not, it's up to you.' She shrugged, got into her car and drove off, leaving him standing on the roadside.

He came about ten minutes after she'd got in.

She'd made the coffee and it was on a tray in the lounge with a plate of biscuits.

'Come in,' she said as she opened the front door to him. 'By the way, I forgot to thank you for changing my tyre. It's something I've never done and would be quite incapable of anyway, as you so rightly surmised.' She gestured expressively.

'If you're ever in that situation again at that time of night, you should lock yourself into your car and you should carry a mobile phone with you.'

'I do have one—that's what I would have done eventually, I guess. Come through,' she invited. 'Coffee's ready.'

He followed her into the lounge, but stood for a moment looking around as if familiarizing himself with it again. Nothing had changed. Then he sat down opposite her in an armchair, and was silent again as she poured the coffee until finally, when she'd given him his and he'd declined a biscuit, she sank onto the settee and looked at him.

'How have you been?'

He moved his shoulders. 'Fine, thank you. And you?'

'The same. Busy, as usual. How…how are your horses and…Lidcombe Peace?'

He didn't answer. And although he was sitting apparently at ease, in his khaki trousers, blue shirt and tweed sports jacket, there was a cutting little glint in his eyes and the line of his mouth was hard. There was also, in the way he was watching her right through to her soul, she felt, the implied cynical disbelief that she could make small talk as if they'd never been as devastatingly and breathtakingly intimate as two people could get.

In fact, as his gaze swept over her she might as well have been in his arms with him pleasing her physically as only he could...

'All right,' she said barely audibly and desperate to break this hold he had over her, 'no more silly platitudes. I left because...'

She paused and glanced at him, then put her cup down on the coffee-table with suddenly shaking hands, and knew it was impossible to tell him the real reason—it hadn't been possible in the first place and it was no different now. How did you tell a man you wanted marriage and children from him and not a purely physical relationship—without baring your soul and laying it open to more pain? Why would he not instinctively know it when he knew everything else there was to know about her, anyway?

'Because...' she swallowed '...nice as it was, Angus, it was...it *was* time for me to move on. Business is booming for me but it's also a critical time, I really need to concentrate and give it my all and...but it had nothing to do with...who you were or who you weren't.'

'And not at all difficult to go from my bed to Emilio Strozzi's?' His expression was now shockingly mocking. 'Perhaps you were able to combine business *and* pleasure in his?'

'I...' She stood up and, to her relief, anger came to her aid. Anger and pride and she didn't care if she was looking arrogant, down her nose or stuck-up as she said coolly, 'That has nothing to do with you, Angus.' She looked at her watch and added, 'I'm sorry, but it's getting late. If you don't mind, there are some preparations I'd like to make for tomorrow.'

She put her cup on the tray and reached for his only to find her wrist clamped in his grasp as he stood up himself. But she refused to make a sound as she straightened and their gazes clashed, although her eyes were blazing.

'You may like to think you can dismiss me like a prospective countess, Domenica,' he said through his teeth, 'but there's one little matter we need to resolve. I wonder if he ever made you feel—as if you were falling…falling through space, as you once told me right here in this room I made you feel?'

Her lips parted.

'I wonder if he knows exactly where you like to be touched, and where, sometimes, the pleasure is so great, you had to tell me to stop. Did you ever dance with him half naked?' His eyes pinned her into immobility and his hand was still hard around her wrist. 'Did he discover that you only ever thought yourself capable of being fulfilled once a night until *we* proved otherwise?'

'That's *despicable*,' she breathed, going from pale to flushed.

'It's also true,' he said roughly. 'Or was it a learning curve you took with me and now intend to practise with other men? You were not particularly—practised when you came to my bed, Domenica, but you did learn fast, I'll give you that.'

A superhuman effort allowed her to wrench her wrist free and slap him. As the blow stung her hand and she realized what she'd done, she paled, though. But as much on account of the act itself as the provocation for it and the stark, awful reality that things could have come to this between her and Angus. And hot, helpless tears welled and started to roll down her cheeks as she put her hand to her mouth in a gesture of anguish.

He stared down at her with a nerve throbbing in his jaw and his teeth clenched, then he closed his eyes and pulled her into his arms.

'Will you marry me, Domenica?'

She stirred and brushed her hair back. She was lying beneath the sheet against her floral pillows and, not only was her bed in disarray, but also her bedroom. There were clothes lying around haphazardly, his and hers—her skirt was still lying on the carpet where she'd stepped out of it.

And if they'd ever ignited each other before it had paled beneath the heights of passion they'd scaled even in misunderstanding and discord. Because the fact was that, although they'd been furiously antagonistic, or, as in her case, desperately sad as well, they had also generated the kind of desire for each other neither had been able to resist.

Where he'd led, she'd followed beneath the sensual onslaught he'd inflicted on her, the devastatingly slow, at times light-as-silk way he'd kissed and touched her, that had drawn from her an aching need, not only for him, but to draw out the same response in him. To need to be released from her clothes so she could slide her slender, curved body against his, to arouse him with her lips and hands and pay tribute to his strength, and their differences that were so glorious, at the same time.

She could never say she'd been taken against her will on this occasion despite their antagonism, because it had faded beneath one clear and stark reality; that what they did to each other was unique for them, and it bound them together—whether they liked it or not.

But it was this last thought that made her answer his question with a question of her own. 'Why?'

He was sitting up; she was lying with her head next to his waist. They were not looking at each other as he started to stroke her hair. 'Isn't that what this is all about?'

She released a careful breath. 'The Strozzis were friends of my father's. Emilio was never invited into my bed, Angus, nor did he get there by other means, although it was what he wanted. I had no idea just being seen in his company would create the storm of publicity it did, nor was there any thought of trying to make you jealous in my mind.'

'I didn't mean that,' he replied quietly, 'although it's a little hard to describe my state of mind when I saw those pictures.' He continued to stroke her hair. 'I meant, isn't that why you went away?'

She still refused to look at him. 'If you could work that out, Angus, I can only conclude it wasn't what you wanted. And I can't think of anything that's changed since then.'

'Yes, it has. If we ever wanted each other, Domenica, we did so only a few hours ago in a way that was...but perhaps I don't have to tell you? Or, to put it another way, can you walk away from us now?'

She shivered involuntarily, and he slid down to be level with her and took her chin gently in his hands as he looked into her eyes. 'I think we have no choice now but to get married or—spend the rest of our lives wanting each other. If you were unable to let an Italian count tread where I had left off, the same thing happened to me. No woman has been worth a second look since you left.'

There was a sort of inescapable logic to this that was, all the same, almost a denial of what she longed to hear. And her eyelids sank beneath the disappointment of it, but he started to kiss them, butterfly kisses that then trailed down her neck and across her bare shoulders until she trembled. Then he lifted his head abruptly and said, 'Hell! It's not as if we only have this in common!'

Her lashes lifted.

And he began to detail, item by item, all the things they'd done together, all the books they'd read, all the music they'd enjoyed, their ongoing, unresolved chess championship, their love of dancing, et cetera, until she couldn't help herself from starting to smile at all the odd little things they'd done that he dug up, including her need of a man in her life who understood waste-disposal units, dryers, et cetera.

It was true, too, she thought, but would marriage change the bigger things he hadn't mentioned? The fact that they'd never made any forward plans for their lives, had never discussed marriage until now, or having children, or even where he'd be at any given time? Perhaps this had been her own fault, perhaps she should have insisted on some of those things instead of living her life and letting him live his unimpeded, as it were.

But what about the biggest one of all? she thought. The knowing, as had happened on Dunk Island, that something was troubling him but not being allowed to share it with him? Would marriage change that? Would there be enough love and trust between them to make having any secrets from the other impossible?

'I don't know,' she said.

He stilled with his lips on the curve of her cheek, then lifted his head to look intently into her eyes.

'But,' she went on, and touched a fingertip to the scar at the end of his eyebrow, 'if you really want to marry me, Angus Keir, I...can't think of what else to do.'

They were married two weeks later.

CHAPTER SEVEN

HER gown was simple and white and she wore a sari-style tulle veil bound with narrow ribbon over her hair to her wedding.

It was hard to gauge her own state of mind as she became Mrs Angus Keir, although she knew they were both tense—she could feel it in his tall frame beside her—but when it was done the joy her mother, sister, Natalie White and her friends expressed for her was reassuring. They, at least, seemed quite sure she was doing the right thing.

And, despite the tension in them, there had been one blinding instant when he'd turned his head to see her on her way up the aisle, when their gazes had clashed and she'd read something absolutely stunned in his eyes.

Despite the short notice, Barbara Harris contrived a marvellous wedding breakfast for them at a restaurant overlooking the harbour and had the time of her life organizing it. She took her daughter aside just before she and Angus were due to leave and told her to be happy because anyone could see that she and Angus were made for each other.

He took her, at her request, to Lidcombe Peace for two weeks' honeymoon. They didn't say much on the drive down, but as soon as they were inside the house he took her in his arms and held her achingly close. Then he said simply, 'I'm honoured, Domenica, and I've never seen you look so beautiful.'

It's going to be all right, she thought, for the second time in relation to Angus Keir as she hugged him back. It's really going to be all right this time.

Nor had she realized how much she'd missed Lidcombe Peace—she hadn't seen it for over three months. And how the tranquillity of it had always soothed her soul without her realizing it before. But not only that—now it was as if Angus was going out of his way to do the same, and their two weeks were like a blessing, she felt, an oasis in their lives during which she could really come to terms with being a married woman, and come to terms with Angus too. It was as if he was concentrating on the small things in their life, as well as the grand and the passionate.

He bought her a puppy, for example, a gorgeous little Blue Heeler she called Buddy that from day one, however, made it plain his chief devotion lay with her husband.

'I get the feeling I'm tolerated, I'm even quite acceptable when you're not around, but otherwise I'm not in the race!' she laughingly told Angus.

'I had one just like him as kid,' he commented. 'We were inseparable.'

'Was this a present for you or me?' she asked severely.

He grinned at her and tickled the pup's fat tummy. 'For both of us. By the way, we are to become proud parents in the near future.'

'I hesitate to contradict you, Angus, but we are not.'

'Well, parents by extension. Josephine is due to be confined shortly and Nap is getting very edgy.'

In fact, the very next day Josephine was confined and they called her baby Elba.

They rode, Angus often with Buddy perched on the saddle in front of him, during those two weeks, they roamed the property from boundary to boundary, they swam in the creek and a glorious burst of weather made every day superb. They also fished in the creek and Angus demonstrated his bush skills by cooking the fish they caught in the hot coals of a fire he'd made.

Domenica dispensed with the couple who looked after the place for the duration of their honeymoon and for the first time gave rein to her Lidcombe genes. Her grandmother had been a great gardener, and she discovered herself to be itching to do some gardening rather than simply giving the orders for what should be done. With Angus's help she dug and planted a herb garden—to satisfy another passion of hers. And she cooked wonderful meals for them and relished having the time to take the trouble.

She also sat down at the piano, often in the evenings, and, after being a little rusty, found all her years of piano lessons plus her mother's music gene coming back to her. Angus seemed to be more than happy to lie back and listen to her playing.

He said to her quite abruptly one night as they sat in front of the fire with Buddy asleep in his basket beside them, 'This wasn't such a bad idea after all, was it?'

She pretended to consider. 'No.'

'You don't sound too sure, Mrs Keir.'

'It's just that it's a little early to be able to judge. But so far so...in fact exceedingly...good.'

'I'm glad you said that otherwise I might have thought you were being a little lukewarm about things.'

She raised an innocent eyebrow at him. 'I wouldn't have thought this was...being lukewarm about anything.'

He had his hands beneath her jumper, under which she wore no bra, and he was warming them on her breasts.

He grinned at her and removed his hands. 'I meant that it wasn't such a bad idea in a more general sense. I don't know about you but I feel very much…married and loving it.'

'So do I. In fact—' she stretched luxuriously '—I feel wonderful!'

He studied her critically. 'You certainly look it.'

So what were the other small things in their life? she found herself wondering once. Actually discussing the future and coming to a joint decision that they would sell his penthouse and her apartment, and buy something new for the time they spent in the city, was one of them. Discussing what kind of electronic equipment she would need to be able to work from Lidcombe Peace when she wanted to was another—neither of them mentioned scaling down their business lives for the immediate future, though.

And they discussed things like putting a tennis court in, taking a trip out west to Tibooburra so she could see where he grew up and, laughingly, how they would cope when they had to be apart.

Then their two weeks were up, they went back to town, consigning Buddy to Luke's care, and a few days later Angus took off on a business trip to the Middle East for ten days. He'd asked her to go with him and she would have loved to, as she assured him, but Natalie was going on holiday. After all the times she'd filled in, often at a moment's notice, Domenica explained that she just couldn't ask her to postpone it—Natalie had made all her bookings for a trip to Vanuatu anyway—and both of them couldn't be away at the same time.

He'd watched her thoughtfully while she'd explained all this, with something she couldn't quite read in his eyes. But it had made her wind down in her explanation rather like a clock that needed a new battery, then stare at him wordlessly.

Before she said abruptly, 'Are you wondering why I wanted to marry you if I can't go on business trips with you?'

He shrugged. 'No. I understand, this all came up out of the blue...' a faint smile touched his mouth '...and can't be helped. But I was wondering whether you always intend to be a career girl?'

She rubbed her brow. 'I haven't really had much time to think about it. No, I guess not, certainly not a full-time career once...once any kids come. But I suppose Primrose, and now Aquarius, are a bit like kids to me.'

'How would it be if we went into partnership?'

She blinked at him. 'In what way?'

'If I bought a share in your business and put in some management, say. You could still design but the day-to-day running of the place, plus all the energy you expend on marketing et cetera, would be taken care of and you'd have a lot more time to be a wife.'

She opened and closed her mouth several times but was quite unable to find a thing to say.

He smiled and touched his fist to the point of her chin. 'Think about it while I'm away, then. It was only a thought.'

'OK...'

'And why don't you start looking for our new place in town?' he suggested.

'Yes. I will. Can I drive you to the airport?'

'If you like, although you don't have to. I...' he paused '...usually take a taxi.'

'Ah,' Domenica murmured, 'but look at it this way—taxi drivers are all very well, but they don't come in and have a cup of coffee with you, nor do they kiss you goodbye—'

'Thank heavens!'

'And they don't have your extreme welfare at heart, your safety in mind, not to mention their own impending sense of loss.'

He took her hand and raised it to his lips. 'It's only ten days.'

'I know,' she said gloomily. 'That doesn't mean to say I won't be miserable.'

'I could put someone in to take over from you right now, Domenica,' he offered.

'Angus, thanks.' She folded his hand around hers and rested it against her cheek. 'I don't think you could, though, and I'm just being silly! But I do reserve the right to drive you to the airport.'

*　　*　　*

She was extremely busy while he was away and, although they spoke to each other daily, she was tense and restless without him. After he'd been away for five of the ten days, she identified the cause of her tension as not solely to do with missing him, but the question of selling him a share of her business.

It sounded so sane and rational. She *was* a wife. She was also a wife whose husband had business interests abroad and travelled a lot. She was the one who had yearned for this marriage, but—and it surprised her what a big 'but' this was in her mind—surrendering any part of her small empire, even to Angus, would be difficult.

It occurred to her that she wanted to have her cake and eat it. But how could she want to have him constantly in her life without being prepared to make any sacrifices for it? Because she still wasn't one hundred per cent sure about his motives for marrying her?

She found herself wondering this, lying in bed one night but unable to sleep.

She got up and made herself a midnight snack with a cool drink, and pursued her internal dialogue. There were all sorts of things to take into account, she told herself. Without the reassurance of his presence, it was natural to be lonely and correspondingly...tilting at windmills, something she was prone to in any case, she thought ruefully. Or at least had been accused of it.

It was also natural to be suffering some re-action. In the space of less than a month she'd gone from heartbreak to intense joy, to being married almost before she'd had a chance to draw a breath, to a lovely honeymoon but, oh, so short, and now, to being alone again. Why wouldn't she be feeling a little shell-shocked?

Unless, she thought, it was the first occasion she'd had the time, and presence of mind, to look past all the passion and glory, even the homeliness of being at Lidcombe Peace with him—to the fact that, without her taking the drastic step of leaving him, he might never have asked her to marry him.

She sighed desolately and took herself back to bed. But the next morning, she managed to convince herself she was simply lonely and missing him terribly and that was what it was all about. That same evening, however, he rang to say that he'd have to extend his trip by a week because of a domestic currency crisis that had thrown the country he was in into turmoil and was having a direct effect on one of his companies.

She reassured him that she was fine and quite understood, but as she put the phone down she found that her first reaction was—nothing's changed!

'Nat,' she said, the day Natalie got back to work after her holiday—Angus was due home in two days' time—'I've been toying with the idea of putting on someone to fill in for me when I can't be here. What do you think?'

'I think it's an excellent idea. Now you're a married lady, you don't want to be working all your life.' She paused and eyed Domenica. 'As a matter of fact I was wondering whether you'd want to quit altogether?'

'No.' Domenica hesitated. 'But we can afford an extra staff member now and I think that should take enough pressure off me for, well, you know!'

'Your wifely duties?' Natalie suggested and they both laughed until Natalie sobered and added, 'Doesn't Angus mind you working?'

'Angus is realistic enough to know that I'd go crazy without something to do and also—' she looked around '—what this all means to me. But I do need to be able to travel with him, and, as you yourself know, that can come up within half an hour!'

'I do,' Natalie agreed wryly, but somehow managed to look sceptical as well.

'What?' Domenica asked.

But Natalie only shrugged and refused to be drawn, saying it was nothing.

Domenica regarded her friend and partner frustratedly. 'He did suggest that he bought a share in the company and put in some management of his own. How would you feel about that?'

'If I had to lose you—'

'I would always design,' Domenica broke in.

'All the same, if it came to having to break up our partnership and find another, I'm sure couldn't go wrong with Angus—yes, I would do it.'

'Hmm,' Domenica commented.

Which was hardly enlightening, Natalie pointed out. She also added, 'He is your husband, Dom.'

'I know,' Domenica said slowly, 'but I'd like to try it my way first, if it's OK with you.'

Her reunion with Angus spoke for itself.

He came back on a Friday and they spent the weekend at Lidcombe Peace in a daze of bliss, as she remarked once.

The remark was prompted by the events that followed as they happened to be getting ready for bed on the Friday evening. And she happened to be wearing the camellia-pink voile dress she'd been wearing when he'd first laid eyes on her.

He mentioned this to her as he stilled her hands on the buttons and appointed himself to the task of undoing them.

'I do remember,' she replied, studying his dark head as he freed each button. 'I also remember how, on that occasion, you looked through this dress as if it simply didn't exist.'

He glanced up with the most wicked glint in his grey eyes and didn't deny the charge. In fact, after agreeing that he'd done precisely that, he added that it was the first time she'd looked down her nose at him.

'Wouldn't you have, in my shoes?' she countered.

He straightened and slid the dress off her shoulders. Beneath it she wore a champagne camisole with a lace front and a matching pair of high-cut briefs.

He said, as the dress slid to the floor, 'I think you have to make some allowances for we poor males of the species, Domenica. On the other hand…' he lifted the hem of the camisole and waited until she stretched her arms above her head '…I'm all in favour of you being at your most haughty and arrogant should any other man but me look at you like that now.'

He pulled the camisole off but she didn't lower her arms immediately, although she linked her fingers above her head.

'I see,' he said gravely, his eyes on the way her breasts had tautened.

'Apart from the obvious, what do you see, Angus?' she asked, with her own wicked little glint.

'That I'm going to be made to pay for my indiscretions—that you fully plan to drive me wild, Domenica, or something like that,' he murmured.

'Something like that,' she agreed huskily, and turned away from him, but only to sit down on their bed, then lie back, and she spread her hair out with her fingers, lifted one leg to point her toe, then lowered her foot to the bed with her knee bent. And looked up at him with something akin to a challenge in the dark blue of her eyes.

He sat down beside her but didn't touch her.

She grimaced, then raised her hips, wriggled out of her briefs and tossed the scrap of lace away.

He put his hand on the slight mound of her stomach, then trailed his fingers down towards the triangle of dark curls at the base of it. 'If I was impertinent that day, I was also right,' he said barely audibly. 'About all the—excellence that lay beneath that pink dress.'

'I don't know about that,' she responded. 'but if it is true, all this excellence is seriously in need of *your* particular brand of excellence before—' she looked at him seriously '—you drive *me* quite wild, Angus,' she confessed ruefully.

They laughed together for a moment, then came together in a way she was later to tell him was pure bliss.

The subject of selling him a share of her business didn't come up until he'd been home for a while.

She showed him all the apartments she'd looked at and was overjoyed when he liked the one she liked best, one right on the harbour with a roof garden. One that, somewhat to her amusement, he immediately bought and told her to decorate as she liked. The penthouse was to be sold furnished, as Angus had bought it, apart from his art collection, and Christy and Ian were considering buying Domenica's apartment.

'Don't you want to have any input?'

He thought for a bit. 'I rather like this room.' He looked around the penthouse den. 'And I'd like a spot in a room like it for my picture. Otherwise it's up to you.'

She'd bought him the painting of the drover for a wedding present and he'd loved it. He'd bought her an oval ruby engagement ring surrounded by a collar of tiny diamonds. She had gasped, and still did sometimes, at the beauty of it.

'OK, well, busy times ahead,' she said. They were having a late supper after a concert, in the penthouse den, of tea and toasted cheese.

'Did you think about my suggestion for Primrose and Aquarius?' he asked idly.

For some reason she took a little breath, then looked at him straightly. 'Yes, I did. But I had another idea.' She told him what it was.

He didn't respond for a moment or two and she watched his long fingers twirling his teaspoon while he stared absently into space. Then he shrugged. 'It's up to you.'

'You just said that,' she pointed out, 'in relation to decorating our new home. Why do I

get the feeling you don't approve of this—*it's*
up to me? Or, am I imagining it?'

He brought his gaze to her face and the
frown on it. And said mildly, 'If you can't let
them go, you can't.'

'Could you let Keir Conway go? By the
way, I've always meant to ask you who the
Conway is?'

'No one in the company. It was my father's
first name.'

'I thought you didn't like your father,
Angus.'

He moved his head and seemed to be con-
templating something rather puzzling. 'He was
still my father,' he said at last. 'And, no, I
couldn't let Keir Conway go, but I'm not the
one who will be attempting to do two jobs.'

'This way, I will be able to do two jobs,
although that's rather an odd description of it,'
she said slowly, and with a little chill running
down her spine.

'Then we have no problem, Mrs Keir.' He
lay back and allowed his heavy-lidded gaze to
play upon her figure in the grey sheath dress
she'd worn to the concert, with her grand-

mother's pearls. 'Why don't you come and sit next to me? I might be able to come up with a better job description.'

She hesitated, then her lips curved. 'I've already been given one for—that kind of thing.'

'Oh?' He looked amused. 'Such as? And who by?'

'Nat. She referred to them as ''wifely duties''.'

'Well—' he laughed softly '—that's one way of putting it. But do you see it as a duty, Domenica?'

'Ah.' She got up, kicked her shoes off and came over to curl up on the settee beside him. 'Not really.' She wrinkled her nose. 'No, I'd put it more in terms of—job-wise—a rather thrilling and challenging occupation.'

'I'm all for the thrilling but what's so challenging about it?' he asked wryly.

She paused. She had her head on his shoulder, and couldn't see his eyes, but she made no attempt to as she said, 'There's the challenge of not knowing what you're really thinking sometimes.'

'I could say the same for you.'

She laughed. 'I thought I was an open book to you! Aren't I?'

'Domenica...' he picked up her hand and twisted the ruby on it '...no, but I don't think we should worry about it or dwell on it. We are individuals and it's probably nice to surprise even your nearest and dearest sometimes.'

She lifted her head and looked at him at last, but was conscious of going into retreat mode—after all, if there were areas he didn't want exposed to her, she had her own no-go zones, didn't she? 'If you say so, Angus. I shall do my best to surprise you from time to time,' she added teasingly, although that little feeling of chill was still with her, but she had no idea how to deal with it now.

'I can imagine. By the way, I've thought of a much better job description. How about designating you as The Fashion Designer Who Invades My Dreams—in capitals, and in the most specific way?'

'I...' she mused, and, suddenly deciding humour was the only way for her to keep going '...well, it's a bit of a mouthful but I...like it.

I've thought of one for you. The Chief Executive Who Makes Me Go Weak At The Knees.'

'Do I?'

'Don't you know it?' she countered.

'I've suspected it occasionally but perhaps I ought to put it to the test, as in right now.'

'Be my guest,' she said softly, but with her eyes alight with mischief.

'You wouldn't be planning to hold out on me for as long as you can?' he asked, looking at her askance. 'You have a certain look in your eye I mistrust devoutly.'

'That will be for you to find out, Angus,' she replied gravely. 'But if you're good enough at the job you may even be promoted.'

'What to?'

'I'll tell you when the time comes, Mr Keir,' she said coolly and stood up. 'The office is this way.' And she walked towards the bedroom, regally ignoring her shoes and purse.

'Tell me.'

'Angus,' she gasped, some time later, 'if

you don't—bring this to a conclusion soon, I might die.'

'I might just die with you,' he said unevenly, 'but I need to know if I'm worthy of a promotion.'

He had brought her, with exquisite sensuality, to the brink several times, only to retreat at the last moment. And what had started in fun in the den had soon seen the tide of their desire run red hot but, she'd realized dimly, with a darker side to it. A contest, in fact, or maybe even a power play. But what was he so determined to get her to admit? she wondered as she shivered beneath his touch and made a husky sound in her throat as he teased her nipples with his teeth.

She pressed her fingers through his hair and gasped, 'Enough, it's too nice, I give in...'

He lifted his head and stared down into her eyes. 'Tell me, Domenica.'

'Yes,' she breathed, 'you've been promoted.'

'To?'

'The...The Husband Of My Heart—in capitals and every other way. Angus, I love you!'

She felt him sigh, then he gathered her close and finally, and powerfully, brought them to the release they were both desperate for.

'Domenica.' He stopped her with a hand on her wrist as they were about to part the next morning, both on their way to work.

They were just inside the front door of the penthouse. He was wearing a fawn suit with a brown shirt and a dark green tie. She was dressed more formally than normal for work, in a straight cornflower linen dress with cinnamon suede accessories and her hair up—she was lunching with a fashion-store buyer.

'Yes?' Her shoes had little heels so she had to look up to him.

'Are you OK?'

'Fine. Why?' Apart from the question in them, her blue eyes were cloudless, although there were the faintest of shadows beneath them.

'Last night was—' he paused '—a little dramatic.'

She moved her slim shoulders. 'I'm not some fragile flower.'

'No,' he agreed rather dryly, 'but I still may have got a bit carried away.'

'I may have had something to do with that,' she said prosaically, although it was far from how she felt, and the unresolved question on her mind was what had it really been all about? Was there some deeper reason behind that tempestuous game they'd played last night? Which she had lost, although in the fiery finale, then the tender aftermath when she'd clung to him and he'd soothed her slim body as well as her mind, it had seemed as if they'd never been closer…

'You did,' he murmured. 'You always do, in fact. But I'm sorry if I did get carried away. May I buy you lunch?' He carried her hand to his lips.

She started. She hadn't told him why she was dressed up. 'Um…actually, I can't. I've got a business lunch. But, may I cook you dinner tonight, Mr Keir? I could even do your favourite meal.'

She'd noted the way his hand had briefly hardened on hers as she'd spoken, and she held her breath. But a slow smile lit the back of his eyes as he said, 'Not hamburgers?'

'Uh-huh. With the works. Just how you like them.'

'It's a date,' he said, and released her hand and bent his head to kiss her gently on the mouth. 'Go safely, Mrs Keir.'

But despite finding their old footing that evening when she made hamburgers and they drank beer with them, and despite the fact that their life seemed to even out after that, somewhere deep in her heart that little chill lingered.

They moved into their new apartment but spent most weekends at Lidcombe Peace. She hired her extra staff member and she travelled with him a lot and loved it, at first. Then they came to a laughing agreement that on purely business trips, when she would be spending a lot of the time on her own, she'd be better off at home.

But as the next couple of months went by, she began to feel as if she were swimming against an unseen tide. She began to really understand for the first time how hard he worked, and how hard it was for him to switch off at times. She saw him roaming around the apartment talking on his mobile phone, sometimes in the middle of the night, then come to bed but be uninterested in discussing anything with her.

Only by accident she discovered that he'd fended off a takeover bid for one of his companies. She read about it in the paper and asked him about it. He shrugged and said it was one of the hazards of going public, that was all.

They did a lot of entertaining, mostly for business and far more than she'd guessed he ever did, so that even with the invaluable Mrs Bush she began to find it quite tiring.

But the other reason that saw her often tired was the fact that her business was literally burgeoning. Even with more new staff hired, she herself was often flat out. It was like a dream come true, or would have been before she'd met and married Angus Keir.

And, without quite knowing how it came about as well as not seeing the danger signs, she began to stay home more and more often when he travelled, and be as preoccupied by work as he was. Although there hadn't appeared to be any danger signs, she was to think sadly after it all blew up in her face. They still ignited each other, they still had so many things in common, they still were more than happy to be in each other's company, they still loved and laughed together. But the fact was, they lived their lives almost exactly as they had before they'd married—in compartments.

And, yes, there had been danger signs, she realized too late, she just hadn't seen them as such. The very first had been what had happened the night she'd told him she would like to keep control of Primrose and Aquarius. Or, no, she found herself musing painfully, had the real damage begun with that shadow at the back of her mind, that uncertainty as to why he had finally married her, and had it led her to be as much at fault as he was?

But the way it all blew up, as so often happened, was over nothing.

'Angus, could you take these people out to dinner tomorrow night? I just don't feel up to putting on a bright face for a bunch of strangers, let alone catering for them. Sorry, darling,' she said whimsically.

They'd just finished their own dinner, which they'd eaten outside in the roof garden of their new apartment where she'd created a leafy wonderland with shrubs, potted lemon and orange trees, soft lighting and some lovely statues, and they'd come inside as a light drizzle had started to fall.

'Let Mrs Bush do it all,' he suggested, looking up from the sheaf of papers he was paging through. 'She always used to do it.'

'I know but…' Domenica hesitated '…I just can't seem to divorce myself from at least helping her.'

'Why don't you take the day off tomorrow, then?'

She stretched. She was curled up in an armchair wearing jeans and a pink blouse and she reached for her coffee-cup. 'I would love to.'

She sipped some coffee, then stifled a yawn. 'But I have one—' she counted off her fingers '—two—at least three meetings tomorrow to do with the launch of Aquarius's little sister, Pisces,' she said humorously. Pisces was the name she'd chosen for the range of children's sportswear she'd branched out into after the outstanding success of Aquarius.

'Domenica.'

She stopped in the act of sipping some more coffee, to look across at him at the unusual tone of his voice. 'Yes?'

'This ''bunch of people'' happen to be important to me. I don't want to take them to a restaurant, I want to entertain them here. So however you do it doesn't much matter, but that's what we'll be doing.'

She put her cup down carefully and stood up slowly. Then, with tears streaming down her cheeks and a sense of horror and disbelief in her heart, she heard herself shouting at him like a fishwife. The salient points of her tirade were that she refused to be ordered around, she was not some employee of his, she was tired of entertaining strangers—in fact, at least before they'd been married, she'd been able to come and go as she'd pleased and it had suited her much better.

He put his papers aside and stood up himself with his mouth compressed into a hard line. 'You know what the problem is?' he said harshly. 'You are tired—you're exhausted because you're doing too bloody much, but what really fails me is *why* you feel you have to do it. It's not as if you need the money or as if the world will be poorer without your efforts.'

She went white beneath the taunt and her mouth worked. 'So what would you have me do instead? Become some sort of sleep-in catering manageress for you?'

'Not at all,' he said grimly. 'As I pointed out, you could leave it all to Mrs Bush—'

'If I'm going to do it I don't want to leave it all to Mrs Bush, I want to imprint some part of myself on what we do here so that at least it feels like a home.' She looked around wildly. 'But when I don't *feel* like it, why should I have to?'

'This—doesn't feel like a home?' he asked dangerously.

'No! And I feel like an unpaid mistress a lot of the time!' Tears were still pouring down her cheeks. 'We never did get to Tibooburra, we never did put a tennis court in at Lidcombe Peace, we have never once discussed having children and, I don't care what you say about surprising one's nearest and dearest, I no more know what your inner thoughts are most of the time than I ever did and I hate it!'

'Because you don't have the time,' he shot back, 'and you won't make the time. How the hell are you going to cope with children if you're so tied up you can't even know what I'm thinking?'

'It's not that!' she cried 'You don't want me to know what you're thinking. There's still a Lone Ranger in you, Angus, I always knew it and don't think I couldn't work out that's why you didn't ask me to marry you before I walked away from you.'

'Well,' he drawled, 'since you have such wisdom, why did you marry me, Domenica?'

'You know why I married you, Angus. The real question is—why did you marry me? When you work out an answer to that, we may be able to decide whether to go on or not. But in the meantime, I'm taking unpaid leave!'

And she walked out, taking only her purse and car keys with her.

He didn't attempt to stop her.

CHAPTER EIGHT

DOMENICA let herself into her old apartment with a sense of unreality and despair.

Christy and Ian, who were due to be married within a month, had asked if they might lease it from her until they could afford to buy it and she'd been more than happy to accommodate them. So it had lain idle in a manner of speaking—Christy was still living with their mother and the leasing wasn't to commence until after the wedding.

It was still basically furnished although all her treasures had either gone back to Lidcombe Peace or the new apartment. The bed was still made up, there were still some clothes in her wardrobe, there were still some groceries in the pantry, although no milk, but she made herself a cup of black tea. And sat down in the lounge to ponder the future.

But all she could think of was that Angus hadn't stopped her from walking out. He'd let her go. Which was what he'd basically done before—made no effort to track her down or get in touch when she'd got home from Europe.

She went to bed eventually and cried her heart out before falling asleep with nothing resolved. But as dawn stole over the park below her windows she sat up and suddenly saw the key to the problem or what she devoutly hoped was the solution.

It took a week to put her plan into action, and she heard nothing from Angus. But she made no attempt to contact him either. Then she went down to Lidcombe Peace and prepared to wait for him for as long as it took for him to come.

He came four days later and it couldn't have been more inauspicious, she was to marvel to herself.

She'd spent the previous three days in a cocoon; she'd gardened, taken long walks with Buddy, she'd tidied out cupboards and done all sorts of housewifely chores with a sense of inner peace that was amazing. Then, on the morning of the fourth day, she decided to mow the lawn—the couple who maintained the place were on holiday and Luke was away for the day.

She had driven the ride-on mower before; Angus had shown her how and it was really very simple. She even knew how to check the petrol and she found the tank full. And it started at the touch of a button. Ten minutes later, she got one front wheel jammed at right angles to its normal direction as she misjudged a ditch between the lawn and a flower bed. No amount of revving or reversing the motor or trying to swing the steering wheel made any impression; in fact the motor died on her, leaving the mower irrevocably stuck at a precarious angle.

She jumped off and tried to push it out of the ditch—it was only a small depression really, but she found that she might as well have been trying to move the Taj Mahal about.

Finally, scarlet in the face, puffing and panting and with tears in her eyes, she tore off her hat and yelled curses at it that caused Buddy to lie down and put his paws over his eyes. And she was just about to kick it when Angus said from close behind her, 'Domenica, that's liable to hurt you more than the mower.'

She swung round and nearly fell over, and all the nervous strain of the past week and a half, capsized her new found serenity as effectively as a tidal wave would swamp a ship.

'Don't you dare laugh at me, Angus Keir,' she warned hysterically. 'And don't think you're much of a husband either, you're never damn well around when I need you!'

'I am here at the moment, Domenica,' he pointed out.

'Yes—' she put her hands on her hips '—here today, gone tomorrow, no doubt. Well, I *don't* need you!' She glared at him.

He studied her thoughtfully, the yellow T-shirt she wore beneath denim dungarees, her boots, the wayward darkness of her hair and the sweat streaks on her face and neck. In contrast he looked cool and formal in a white business shirt, charcoal trousers and a blue and grey Paisley tie.

'The mower might need me, however,' he murmured. And with very little effort he righted the wheel, pushed it out of the ditch and pressed the starter button. It sprang to life. 'I think you probably flooded it earlier.'

She closed her eyes and ground her teeth, then turned her back on him and strode up to the house. She heard him drive the mower back to the garage and it was a good five minutes before he came to find her, sitting on the veranda. Five minutes during which she'd started to calm down and be appalled at what she'd done.

He came round the corner of the house and stopped at the table where she was sitting with her feet up on an opposite chair. But neither of them said anything for a long moment. She, because she was drinking in everything about him and being affected by it in a way that made her mouth go dry and her heart pound. He looked as physically impressive as always, but she thought he was paler than his usual tan and wondered whether it was her imagination or if there were new lines beside his mouth.

Then she looked away and said, 'Sorry, but you probably know how—excitable some things can make me so perhaps I could start again—hi!'

'Hi.' He paused. 'Yes, I do.'

She shrugged.

'You also look hot.'

She nodded, lost for words, unable even to move somehow and supremely uncertain of whether she'd lost Angus Keir for good and if this might be their last farewell.

'Can I buy you a cool drink?'

'Yes, please. I'll wait here.' She finally found her tongue. 'I'm a bit grubby.'

'I'll get it.'

She fanned herself with her hat and in a few minutes he brought out a tray with two tall frosted glasses of juice and a packet of biscuits.

'Thanks.' She picked up a glass and took a long swallow. 'You probably didn't expect to see me here, Angus, but—'

'I knew you were here.' He sat down opposite her.

She looked fleetingly surprised.

'Luke kept me informed, but in fact I've known where you were ever since you left.'

'But...' She stopped confusedly.

'I had a few things to do,' he said. 'May I tell you about them?'

She caught her breath. 'Angus, there's something I'd like to tell you first and—please don't take too much notice of what I said earlier. You know what I'm like.'

'Domenica...' his grey eyes rested on her sombrely '...yes, but I'd like to speak first.'

A feeling of dread gripped her at that look in his eyes. 'I would rather—'

'No.' He slid a hand across the table to cover hers. 'I need to tell you that, for the first time in my life, I can understand my father.'

She stared at him wordlessly.

'Because, twice in my life now, I've experienced the same sense of loss he did, that seems to freeze your soul over and leave you feeling as hard as shatter-proof glass. And about as vulnerable inside as normal glass. But I now know why he was that way. Because, for all their differences and who was right and who was wrong, he loved my mother in a way that wouldn't let him love anyone else, or forget her. And I could see it at last, because the same thing had happened to me.'

Domenica licked her lips and felt her heart start to beat differently—not so much like a muffled drum now.

'The other problem I've always had,' he went on, 'is the inability to place my ultimate trust in anyone else, no doubt compounded by the way my life was. So, yes, up until very recently the ''Lone Ranger'' was alive and well in me, as you so accurately pointed out.'

She grimaced and drew a pattern on the side of her glass with a fingertip. 'I tried to make allowances for all that but—' she looked at him suddenly '—it's been almost impossible not to think that all you wanted or needed from me was…was…' She couldn't go on.

'Your body?' he said softly.

'Yes.' She closed her eyes. 'It has been such a physical thing between us at times. Was that why, in your heart of hearts, you didn't want to marry me? So that we could keep it like that instead of—wearing it out, perhaps?'

'No. And I did want to marry you in my heart of hearts, I just couldn't help feeling—' He paused and sighed. 'I swore once I'd never put myself in the position my father found himself in.'

She couldn't speak and she felt herself starting to tremble.

'But,' he went on, 'during these last days, after I couldn't bring myself to do what I really wanted to do that last night—do *anything* to stop you from going—and as that awful hardness started to take over again, I knew I had to fight it and fight to keep you. So this is what I did.'

She listened in growing, stunned silence because what he'd done was virtually reorganize his empire. He'd even appointed a managing director in his place, although he would still hold the position of president of the company. And, although he would still ultimately hold the reins, the business side of his life would be scaled down considerably.

'I have to be honest and say, as I told you once before—' he smiled faintly '—that for quite a time now it's what I've wanted to do.

There's been a siren song in my heart for a better life than being on the end of a phone all the time, getting on and off planes, or brokering business deals. I had the feeling it was the time to move on.'

He hesitated and looked around. 'It was why I bought this place, but there was still something missing, although it slowly began to dawn on me around about the same time as I got Lidcombe Peace what that siren song might be—you. Only, I didn't have the courage to think I could hold you, Domenica.'

She wiped a tear off her cheek with her wrist.

'But, at the same time, would I be wrong in saying you've always had your secret reservations about us? Even ones that you didn't tell me about that last night?' he asked gently.

'What do you mean?' she whispered.

'I kept thinking, after we were married, that there was only one reason for you to want to hold onto Primrose, et cetera, and work so hard—you wanted to keep it as an escape hatch?'

She flinched visibly and looked briefly out across the roses towards Sydney.

'And, I have to confess,' he said a little grimly, 'that it activated all my old doubts. Doubts that raised their head with me when you were too independent to accept a car from me.'

She looked back at him at last. 'No, you wouldn't be wrong, Angus,' she said barely audibly. 'I did think of it as an escape hatch but only because—can I tell you something? Do you know when I first knew I wanted to marry you? When you gave me that car for my birthday rather than an engagement ring.'

'So *that*…' His hand tightened over hers and his grey eyes narrowed.

'That's why I made such a fuss. Then,' she said huskily, 'I knew there was more to Dunk than "island magic". I could sense—' she gestured with her free hand '—it was as if you were at a crossroad and I thought it might be over me—'

'It was.' His eyes were bleak now.

She wiped her nose. 'But nothing came of it and I couldn't believe that we could be so close and not be taking that final step. Then I found out that Christy was secretly engaged to Ian and I woke up one morning with a rosebud on my pillow, but alone. Silly little things but they were the straws that broke the camel's back. And that's why I left.'

'But you couldn't tell me these things?'

'No. If you had your fears, Angus, I've also had mine.'

'Were they anything at all to do with giving yourself completely to a boy from the bush?' There was a glint of sudden humour in his eyes, but it didn't strike an answering chord in her.

'You don't still believe that of me, do you, Angus?'

The glint disappeared. 'I sometimes watch the way you walk and talk, the way you are with people, the way you light up a room with your presence and grace and humour, your essentially well-bred composure—and I sometimes think there's an ultimate reserve in you I could never break through. And I remember that I didn't own my first suit until I was twenty-two and it was a second-hand one.

Sometimes, I can't help wondering if there's a connection.'

Domenica closed her eyes again because she was more moved than she'd ever been in her life. 'The only ultimate reserve in me,' she said barely audibly, 'is the fear that you don't love me the way I love you. That's why I clung to Primrose. I could never quite shake the shadow of why you hadn't asked me to marry you long before you did, and I couldn't help feeling, once we were married, that nothing had changed, that marriage had even divided us.'

Her lashes fluttered up. 'But I came to my senses and finally saw what I was doing. So, I've also...done some rearranging, Angus. I didn't tell you this but I got an offer to buy out my share of Primrose a few weeks ago and—I've now sold.'

He made a harsh sound and got up abruptly to come round the table to her. 'You didn't have to.'

'Yes, I did,' she said serenely. 'Natalie is happy with the new partner and I'll still design for them but I had to let you know, whether you still wanted me—or not, that there were

no more escape clauses for me and no more
attempts to be a part-time wife.'

He pulled her up into his arms and held her
desperately close for a long time. 'Whether I
still want you is not an issue, Domenica,' he
said unevenly. 'I always will. So—' he lifted
his head to look into her eyes '—it seems
we're of one mind at last. But I can't tell you
how awful I feel about being so bloody stupid
for so long, and forcing you to do this,
though.'

She touched her finger to the scar at the end
of his eyebrow. 'Don't. When the time came
to sign the last document I felt like a new person. I hadn't realized what a weight it had all
become—even apart from how it was keeping
us apart. And how I was finding less and less
time, and inspiration, to do what I really love
doing and that's designing.'

'I still feel terrible for being stupid and blind
and self-centred for so long.'

She kissed him. 'Angus, you achieved so
much and you did things so tough as a kid, it
would have been a miracle if there hadn't been
some price to pay. But, if it gets tough for you

again and the past is hard to slough off, just remember you've got me and I *love* you.'

'What's so funny?' he asked, quite a lot later.

Their lovemaking had been different again, as intense as ever but bringing them closer in mental unity than they'd ever been before as they'd told each other things they'd never said before. And revelled in the freedom to do so. Then, when they'd quietened, she'd started to laugh softly.

She stroked his bare shoulder and moved sensuously against him beneath the sheet. 'I'm just meditating upon the fact that my famed composure has now deserted me twice in one day.'

'Ah.' He glinted a wicked look down at her. 'Well, I long ago realized that waste-disposal units, lawnmowers and the like didn't bring out the best in you—in fact, that you really couldn't be held responsible for your actions in relation to them.'

She laughed again and he slid his fingers through her hair and kissed her cheek. 'That also strikes you as funny?' he queried.

'Yes,' she conceded. 'Because the one thing that I really can't be held responsible for are my actions in relation to you. But I'm also thanking heaven I didn't send you away thinking I hated you earlier on.'

They were lying facing each other on the pillow and he put his hand on the slender column of her neck. 'I love you even when you're kicking lawnmowers. I love you even more, if that's possible, when you're all worked up and spitting fire. As for the second time you lost your famed composure today—'

She trembled.

'Would that have been about twenty minutes ago, in this bed, in my arms?'

'Yes, Angus, but then I've never had any composure when you set your mind to wreck it.'

'Domenica—' He stopped suddenly and held her hard. 'Do you know what I did after you walked out?'

'No…'

'I rang up a friend of mine and I arranged with him to fly me to Tibooburra at first light the next morning, and I went to see my father's grave. I went back to see it all. Then I flew to Newcastle, where my mother is buried, and I told them both that their seed would live on in me, and in you, even if I had to move heaven and earth to get you back. And that all the tragedy and loss of their lives and my early life would be reversed in ours, like a desert coming to bloom at last. Because you, and what *you* do to me, make you the one person I couldn't live without.'

Domenica swallowed a lump in her throat but couldn't hide the tears in her eyes. 'Thank you for that. Oh, Angus—' she was suddenly so radiant, he drew an unsteady breath '—I once thought you'd made a new woman of me but that was nothing to this!'

It was the middle of the afternoon when they strolled outside. They'd showered together and because she felt like a new woman she'd put on one of her favourites, a scarlet top with narrow straps and a long, lovely full skirt. It was an outfit that always made her feel carefree and happy. Her hair was loosely tied back, her feet were bare, but she slipped on her engagement ring which she hadn't worn for a week and a half. It was a beautiful afternoon, blue, gold and green.

'It looks like a whole new world,' she said wonderingly.

'It looks to me like a kingdom, and well named. And you—' he looked down at her '—are my quintessential mysterious Indian princess and wild gypsy girl all rolled into one in that dress. You look stunning.'

She swung her arms. 'I feel stunning, thanks to you. You know, I once, in just about this very spot, thought that you wouldn't make a bad Sheik of Araby.'

He looked down at himself ruefully. He was wearing jeans and his khaki bush shirt.

'It's not anything to do with clothes,' she said. 'It's sheer sex appeal. And, although I was a little annoyed at the time, it didn't fail to hit me.'

'You mean—the first time we met?' He raised an eyebrow at her.

'I do,' she said gravely

'You didn't show it—then.'

'That's because I'd only just met you.' She composed her features and looked down her nose at him.

But when they'd stopped laughing, he said, 'I know I did this once before, with disastrous consequences, but these roses are the real thing.' And he broke off a perfect Peace rose and handed it to her.

She took it and breathed in the fragrance. Then she lifted her face to his and said simply, 'Peace—and love.'

He took her hand. 'Peace and love, Domenica,' he agreed.

MILLS & BOON® PUBLISH EIGHT LARGE PRINT TITLES A MONTH. THESE ARE THE EIGHT TITLES FOR JUNE 2001

ALL NIGHT LONG
Anne Mather

THE MARRIAGE RISK
Emma Darcy

A SEDUCTIVE REVENGE
Kim Lawrence

BY MARRIAGE DIVIDED
Lindsay Armstrong

THE PREGNANT BRIDE
Catherine Spencer

THE TYCOON'S MISTRESS
Sara Craven

THE MAN SHE'LL MARRY
Susan Fox

MIDNIGHT WEDDING
Sophie Weston

MILLS & BOON®

Makes any time special™